THE STALKER IN THE DESERT

THE STALKER IN THE DESERT

COLLEEN HOFSTADTER HLAVAC

For my mother, Astrid Hofstadter, who has always been by my side and supported me unconditionally.

1

He sat on the edge of the river bank as the sun was beginning to set. The day had been unusually hot and, finally, there was a reprieve from the sweltering heat. His feet dangled into the cool, rushing water. He recalled how since he was a young boy, the night had always been his favorite time. He still loved vanishing into the darkness and he relished the anonymity the cloak of darkness provided. He whistled and eased himself back onto the grass. He was deeply absorbed in his thoughts. It had been too long, far too long. He wasn't sure how much longer he could hold off on his impulses. His hands longed to surround another delicate neck and feel the life draining from his victim's body. He had killed many times in the past. Each killing gave him an indescribable feeling of power and euphoria. Unfortunately, his favorite activity had been placed on an indefinite hold.

He saw a couple strolling hand in hand in the distance. They looked care free and happy. The temptation to attack them rose within him. He couldn't be foolish. His slayings were always planned down to the last detail. No amount of pleasure he might derive from a random murder would be worth destroying his perfect record. Patience was the key, at this point. He consoled himself,

"The time will come again for you to get the pleasure of ending a life. You will know when it is right but the time is certainly not now. When the opportunity finally presents itself, it will have been worth the wait." The thought soothed him and he gazed, with a renewed calmness, at the dazzling blanket of stars above. It appeared as if someone had tossed diamonds into the sky. They reminded him of fireworks celebrating in the mid summer sky. The moon cast an ethereal glow. It had the power to calm his dark thoughts, at least for the moment. He stretched and yawned and then entered a deep slumber on the river bank's meadow.

2

The day started just like any other. The alarm blared similar to an urgent firehouse siren into Cosette's ear and startled her out of much needed slumber. She stretched and started to embark on her usual morning routine. There was an imprint next to her in the queen-size bed she shared with Chad, her husband. He had been sleeping there only moments before. Cosette threw back the tacky animal print. The fleece material was increasingly pilling. Chad had insisted on purchasing this set last winter despite her preference for a more feminine, silky to the touch, floral, Pottery Barn print.

Spencer, her adorable four year old, was already waiting for his breakfast. Cosette began to make Spencer's favorite, extra crispy bacon and poached eggs. The pots and pans clanged and bumped together as if a freight train was rapidly approaching. The wafts of frying bacon and eggs poaching was definitely a welcoming scent and it was also appetite inducing. Spencer inhaled every bit off of his plastic, cocker spaniel shaped plate within minutes. His hardy appetite never failed to amaze her.

"You eat like a bear who has just come out of hibernation." They both laughed at the truth behind the statement. After breakfast, Cosette drove Spencer to his preschool. He tried to exit the car before it had even come to a complete halt.

"Whoa there, partner. Safety always comes first. Please be patient and wait until the car has stopped."

"I can't wait, Mommy. Chase promised to show me his worm collection this morning. I'm so excited."

"Well, have fun, buddy. I'll see you this evening. I love you so much!"

After Spencer happily disembarked, Cosette sped off in her glossy, wine red convertible VW Bug. She threw on her knock off, Chanel sunglasses and quickly and skillfully tied a ribbon around her long, silky locks. Driving with the top down gave her a feeling of freedom and peace. She loved how her tied back hair whipped around her shoulders. She bathed in the gentle morning sun. Passing the bakery every morning was her favorite part of driving to work. The smell of fresh croissants and chocolate confections made her mouth water.

Her work day was unremarkable. The regular customers came in for their usual purchases of milk, cigarettes, sweet rolls, Jack Daniels and lottery tickets. She made small talk with customers and dutifully rang up their purchases. At last, she was in the final hour of her shift at the convenience store. The weather had taken a dramatic turn since this morning.The rain was gently hitting the fogged up, grease smudged window near her register. Rain showers were regular visitors in her hometown of Seattle, Washington. She would just have to drive home with the top of her car up. Many residents considered this weather gloomy and dreary. Cosette took a certain solace in its predictability. It calmed her and allowed her to get lost in her thoughts as the cloud filled sky above continued to spill onto the beautiful northwestern city.

Finally, 5:00 p.m. arrived. Cosette clocked out and headed to the Joyful Days Pre School to pick up her eternally energetic and, at times, mischievous son. He cheered and ran into her arms as she entered the old schoolhouse.

"Spencer, how was your day?"

"It was great, Mommy. I even got to play with the baby turtles and Ms.Lorraine gave me an oatmeal cookie at snack time. The best part was when Chase showed me his worm collection. They were awesome. Many of them even had dirt on them still. I want a worm collection. Can I, Mom? Please, please?" Cosette used her typical stall technique so as not to disappoint her son.

"We will just have to see, honey." Her statement was enough to distract him and thankfully move him towards other topics.The young boy continued to describe the day's events to his weary mother.

It was a short, seven minute drive to their cozy, modest home. Water droplets assaulted their windshield. The wipers were having a difficult time keeping up with the high level of rain.

"Mommy, it's like we are in a submarine. So cool!" Cosette did not share in his enthusiasm and was laser focussed on getting them both home safely. As usual, her husband, Chad, was not at home, yet. Their marriage could never be described as magical even by the biggest stretch of the imagination but lately he came home from his accounting firm job late into the night, crept quietly into the bed they shared and departed the house again moments before Cosette's alarm sounded at 7:00 a.m. Their communication level had dwindled down to nothing.

After preparing a salad and Spencer's favorite dinner, mac and cheese, the twosome curled up in the cozy, dimly lit family room. Spencer was mesmerized by the show, The Painted Dragon. His focus on the show allowed Cosette to check the emails on her phone without distractions. She turned to look back at the television and could not figure out the fascination children had with the good natured, always upbeat dragon who bounced around playing ping pong and swimming all day. At least, this dragon was temporarily an ideal babysitter while Cosette checked her email messages. As she scanned her inbox, what she saw was long awaited and sent shivers of delight up and down her spine. The email was from World Connect Airlines and the title stated, "An offer of training." As Cosette scanned the email, it quickly became apparent that her lifelong dream was finally coming true. For years, her dream was to be hired by a major airline as a flight attendant. This letter confirmed that they were offering her the first of September as her training date. She was given detailed instructions. She must report to Chicago on the 31st of August and her orientation would begin the following morning at 8:30 a.m. sharp. She was beside herself with a mixture of excitement, apprehension and complete jubilation. Chad had always frowned upon her lifelong goal and he insisted that it was very difficult to get hired by a major airline. He was convinced that she didn't have the poise or customer service skills to get accepted, much less to thrive in her dream career. Many of their conversations about her career aspirations ended in wall shaking screaming matches.

"Cosette, you've got to be the most delusional woman I know. You barely finished high school. You are lucky you even got hired at that two bit convenience store. These airlines get thousands of applications. They will take one look at your credentials, or lack thereof, and your application will be put through the shredder." With the negative memories flashing in her mind, she felt she needed to pinch herself that she was, despite Chad's nay saying, one of the lucky ones to receive the offer of training at this coveted, international airline. Boy, was she going to show Chad. As soon as he walked into the front door, Cosette sprung the good news on him. He was disgusted and reminded her that she would only make a fool out of herself. The frozen tundra was more welcoming and warm than their marriage. With that, he stormed into the bedroom and that was the last interaction they had for days.

3

The following month was a whirlwind of activities for Cosette. She resigned from her job and prepared for her long awaited training. It was difficult to leave her son for two months. She knew that would be the most trying part of fulfilling her dream. Chad seemed indifferent about her upcoming departure date. Their communication continued to dwindle as time passed. She felt as if they were two strangers sharing a home, with Spencer being the last tie they shared.

August 31st finally arrived. Chad and Spencer drove her to the Seattle-Tacoma International Airport. She hugged Spencer and, for a moment, feared she would not be able to let go of him and actually board her flight. Her inner voice reminded her that she had dreamed and prepared for this day for as long as she could remember. Accepting this job would benefit her son as well. She was barely making minimum wage at the convenience store. More often than not, Chad and Cosette had to scrape every last dime together to pay their monthly bills. They never had any extra spending money. They bought their clothes at thrift stores and they rarely enjoyed meals at restaurants or even went on vacations. This job would not only help their finances, but after her six month probation period, Cosette, Chad and Spencer would all be able to travel anywhere in the world for just a minimal fee. That was a benefit Cosette would enjoy immensely. She loved to travel but she had only been on a plane a few times in her life. A weekend trip to camp on the beach was considered a luxury during her childhood. Her parents had always earned modest incomes as well. The list of places she planned on visiting with Spencer were pages long. She was determined to visit all the locations of her dreams with her son. Her ultimate destinations included Bora Bora, New Zealand, Switzerland and Costa Rica. Her goal was for Spencer to see more of the world than she had in her childhood.

When the wheels touched down in Chicago, Cosette felt a lump form in her throat. This was it. It was the beginning of a huge adventure. She took the shuttle and she arrived at the World Connect Airlines Training Center only a short time later. Cosette was told by a business like lady in her late 40's that she was staying in room 794. As she entered her room, both her roommates had already claimed their beds and they were introducing themselves to each other. They beamed as she entered the room and they warmly greeted her. The pleasant looking brunette introduced herself as Maggie from Des Moines, Iowa, and the petite blonde was named Christy. She was from Eugene, Oregon. They spent the remainder of the evening becoming acquainted with each other and preparing for their orientation the following morning. Becoming a flight attendant had been lifelong goals for Maggie and Christy as well. Starting training felt so dream like for all three of the roommates.

4

The next two months consisted of both classroom and online training. Cosette especially enjoyed the actual inflight training. She worked as a trainee on flights to Washington D.C, New York City and even Los Angeles. Cosette enjoyed the work. She loved meeting the different crew members she worked with and chatting with the passengers. Maggie and Cosette were inseparable. She was the best friend Cosette had ever had. They often worked training flights together and they prayed they would end up being based together after training in the same domicile. One month into the training, she was able to go home for a day and spend time with Spencer. She missed him every second of every hour. They spent the time having their own special date. She took him to a local amusement park. They ate cotton candy and giggled nonstop. Their belly muscles ached from the constant laughter they shared together. He clung on to her extra tightly while they were on the mini roller coaster. Cosette loved holding him. Her son was her life. She ached when she wasn't with him. With a heavy heart, she flew back to Chicago the next morning.

A week after she retuned from visiting her son, Cosette's class was called into a large meeting room. The room was sterile and equipped with several ceiling fans, long formica conference tables and an overly robust air conditioning unit which ran endlessly despite it being a frigid October day in Chicago. The head instructor announced that their class was finally assigned to a domicile. The good news was that the entire class would go to the same base. This was already a huge relief to the students because they were determined to stick together as a team and as a support system for each other. At this point, the trainees were actually more like family members than fellow classmates. They each tried to guess which base they were going to be assigned to. Finally, when the suspense was unbearable, the instructor started writing the airport code of the assigned base onto the chalkboard. He wrote, RNO, which stood for Reno, Nevada. Her classmates' responses were a mixture of excitement and dismay. Cosette and Maggie were relieved that they were at least based together even though Reno was somewhat far from both of their homes. Cosette and Maggie decided they would commute on days off to their homes, which meant renting and sharing a "crash pad" in a hotel room. Maggie was single and still lived at her parent's home. She also had two sisters. Julia was the younger sister. The other sister, Samantha, was Maggie's identical twin. They were a close knit family and they had a tendency to be inseparable. When Maggie showed her family photos, Cosette was unable to tell Maggie and her twin, Samantha, apart. Due to the twins close bond, commuting back and forth to Des Moines, for now, made the most sense for Maggie as well. She feared she would become too homesick, at least until she became more accustomed to the Reno area.

The day of flight attendant training graduation was a very proud and happy day for Cosette. After graduation, the entire class had one week off before they were expected to report to their new base. Maggie took the first flight back to her family. Cosette immediately flew home to Seattle. After she disembarked from her flight, she saw a small figure running eagerly to her from the distance. As the figure sprinted closer to Cosette, it became apparent that it was Spencer, her beloved son. They raced into each others arms and clung to each other. Cosette never wanted to let go.Chad approached her moments after and stated in a cold tone,

"Hey there, welcome home." They did not hug or share any kind of physical affection. In under thirty minutes, they were back at their family home. They splurged and ordered Door Dash and enjoyed a savory Chinese dinner. After dinner, Chad briskly excused himself and went to work on the computer in their master bedroom. Spencer exclaimed,

"Mommy, since daddy has so much work to do, why can't we have a sleepover. Please? I'll even let you sleep on the top bunk!"

"Now that sounds like a plan but not before we have a pillow fight, watch a bunch of movies and have extra buttery popcorn".And, that is just what they did.

Cosette kept Spencer out of preschool for the week so she could maximize her time with him. Her week off was over in the blink of an eye. Chad barely acknowledged her when she came home for her break. He was cold and clearly disinterested. She had grown accustomed to his condescending ways but she remained cordial to him for the sake of their son. Shortly before she left for the airport to fly to Reno, Chad served her divorce papers. She was packing up her clothes and he silently handed her a large envelope. When she asked him what the paperwork was, he did not reply and he casually exited the room. Cosette opened the envelope and examined the contents. Cosette was stunned. The divorce papers had broken her heart. She had seriously considered ending the marriage for a couple of years herself. However, for the sake of Spencer, she was determined to stick with the commitment she had made. Sadly, the option of remaining in the marriage had now been taken from her. Upon further reflection, she began to realize that there were some positive aspects to proceeding with the divorce. His cold demeanor and verbal abuse had become too much for her. What was even worse, was that it was setting a horrible example for Spencer. In addition, their son deserved to live in a happy, loving and low stress environment. She wanted to do what was best for her son. He was all that mattered to her. She knew she needed to sign the papers and proceed with the filing process.

5

With a mixture of sadness and excitement she landed in Reno and joined her flight attendant training class at their new base. Cosette and Maggie stayed at the Dreamland Hotel located near the airport.They filled each other in on every detail of their vacation week. Maggie's days were filled with designer clothing shopping trips with her sisters, and binge watching reality shows. She too had enjoyed the time off. Now they were both ready to embark on their new careers. They felt so fortunate to have each other to lean on. The duo attended orientation and then they were immediately assigned to work flights to

Philadelphia, Kansas City and San Francisco. They even worked the same round trip flight to Boston. It was a thrill to be able to work the meal and beverage cart together. They had a great routine and worked well as a team. If it were up to the friends, they would work every trip together. After flights, they watched shows and movies together and drank themselves to the bottom of many rum bottles. They laughed and gossiped and relished their new lives as flight attendants.

During Cosette's third week working at her new job, she was assigned to work in first class from Reno to New York City. She then returned to Reno after an eighteen hour layover in the Big Apple.The flight to New York was uneventful. During boarding, on the return flight to Reno, an extremely handsome passenger boarded and seated himself into a First Class seat. Cosette's breath was taken from her the moment they made eye contact. Her pulse quickened and her palms began to sweat. She estimated that he was in his thirties. He was at least 6'3 and he had a shocking amount of chestnut brown, thick hair. His emerald, almond shaped eyes were hypnotizing. Cosette took a deep breath and composed herself. The flight took off without delay and once the 767 reached an altitude of 20,000 feet, she commenced with her dinner service. It was a full flight and Cosette soon became engrossed in her task of serving a four course meal to a packed First Class cabin. Passengers commented on how perfectly braised the lamb was and they requested cocktail refills. She had discovered that the name of the handsome mystery man in 3B was Luke Meier. Despite his striking and rugged good looks, he also appeared down to earth and kind. He spoke politely to Cosette and his eyes contained a subtle warmth and softness to them. His square jawline, dimpled cheeks and broad shoulders only added to his good looks. After dinner, the cabin lights were dimmed. The majority of the passengers were resting, at this point. Luke asked for another glass of Pinot. Cosette promptly delivered the drink to him. He struck up a conversation with her. He asked where her base was and for how long she had been flying. When he discovered that she was based in Reno, his eyes lit up with excitement.

"Since you have only been flying for a few weeks, I am assuming you have not visited nearby Virginia City?" Cosette's interest was piqued.

"No. In fact, I haven't even heard of that town." Luke responded,

"You don't know what you are missing. It is about a half hour drive from Reno. I'm the owner of a restaurant and bar located directly on the main street. Here, I will give you my card. I'd love to show you around the town on your next days off."

"Oh, I'd love that. I normally fly back to see my son on days off but since I only have one day off on Thursday, I will stay in the area."

"You have a son? How nice. How old is he?"

"Yes, his name is Spencer. He is four years old. He is in preschool. Do you have any children?"

"Nope, single as can be." They both awkwardly chuckled at his response.

"Well, Cosette, I look forward to showing you around my town. I'll see you on Thursday then. I can come pick you up at your hotel at about 2:00 p.m?"

"That sounds perfect," confirmed Cosette.

6

The flight landed. Luke and the remainder of the passengers disembarked. Cosette went back to the hotel and burst into the room she shared with Maggie.

"Maggie, you need to hear about the flight I was just on."

"Do tell. I'm all ears!"

"I met this gorgeous and sweet first class passenger. He owns a restaurant and bar in Virginia City. That is a town about a half hour from our hotel. I am going to visit him on Thursday."

"Are you serious, Cosette?"

"Do I look like I'm kidding?" The friends laughed and continued to catch up on the day's events until they finally both fell asleep in a state of utter exhaustion.

Thursday felt like it arrived in a fraction of a second. In the morning, Cosette went to a nearby candle shop. The shop was small and stuffy. The scent of the candles overwhelmed her senses. She purchased an exotic, jasmine scented candle. She wanted to take a bath before her get together with Luke. She knew it was irresponsible to have an open fire in a hotel room but Cosette never shied away from taking risks. In fact, during her school days, she was known to be a bit of a risk taker. Next, she visited a local florist and bought a dozen red roses. She was in the mood to pamper herself today. She deserved it after her last few grueling flights. She went back to the hotel and started to fill the oversized, jetted tub with water about as hot as she could possibly handle. She sprinkled a midnight oil throughout its watery depths. Then she added a jasmine bubble bath. She picked up some of the foam and blew it. The foam reminded her of billowy clouds. This made her laugh and the thought instantly relaxed her. She lit her beautiful candle and placed it on the edge of the tub. She popped a bottle of champagne and gave herself a generous helping. As a final touch, she sprinkled the fragrant, red rose petals throughout her masterpiece of a bath. She cautiously lowered herself into the steamy, highly fragrant water. She wasn't quite sure why she had so many butterflies in her stomach.After all, she was still a married woman with a young son, no less. Besides, Luke had not given her any indicators that he was romantically interested in her. They were embarking on a new, strictly platonic, friendship, Cosette kept reminding herself of this, in hopes of bringing her pulse down into a somewhat healthy range.

As she exited the oversized, marble tub, she threw her long, luxurious, caramel colored locks into the hotel's Turkish bath towel .She glanced into the magnifying mirror and determined there was work to be done before Luke's arrival. Cosette had always been a modest young woman. She looked in the mirror and genuinely believed there were flaws when, in actuality, her skin was a gorgeous, dewy canvas of peaches and cream. Her large, feline like, green/blue eyes sparkled with a childlike innocence, yet, they were curiously bewitching as well. She proceeded to put a moderate amount of makeup on. A tinted moisturizer, subtle plum colored eyeliner, two coats of the blackest mascara, and a soft, light pink gloss which only emphasized her flawless, bee stung lips.Next, she went to her closet.

"Hmmmm, what should I wear? Well, it is a day time meeting and we are going to an old, silver mining town." She decided on tight jeans which emphasized her never ending, shapely legs and a plain white tee shirt which clung insistently to her delicate curves. Standing at 5'8, it was widely know by coworkers, friends and family that Cosette's physique rivaled even the highest paid supermodels. She pulled her hair out of the towel and it cascaded more than half way down her neatly pressed white top. Cosette and Maggie enjoyed a hot minestrone soup and buttered ciabatta bread together while gazing over the Reno skyline with the snow tipped mountains soaring in the backdrop. Maggie begged, "I would really feel better if I could at least meet this mystery man before you go traipsing off with him for the afternoon."

"That goes without saying, Maggie. And, by the way, we are not "traipsing" off anywhere. He is just a kind man who wants to introduce me to the town he grew up in. I read about Virginia City last night. It sounds fascinating. It is a silver mining town and it even has a history of being heavily haunted. That's right up my alley." Just then, an assertive knock came from their hotel room door. Maggie rushed to answer it. She was taken aback when she saw Luke standing there. Cosette had mentioned he was a good looking man but this was a whole different level. "He was gorgeous!" She invited him in. Cosette, Maggie and Luke talked for about ten minutes. Maggie, despite being Cosette's best friend, couldn't help but feel a twinge of jealousy. Maggie had not had a boyfriend in at least a year and here Cosette was, still legally married, albeit in a loveless marriage, and she had the honor of going out with a stud like Luke.

"Life just isn't always fair," thought Maggie miserably.Luke and Cosette exited for their outing and Maggie was left sitting in the dusky room staring blankly out towards the mountains. Her melancholy continued for the remainder of the day. A dark, foreboding cloud had settled over her.

Luke and Cosette bounded out into the cloudless, sunny day. She followed him to his black Jeep.

"Very nice, Luke. I like it."

"The Jeep is great for off roading. Thats pretty important in this area since we get a lot of snow," responded Luke. Their thirty minute drive to Virginia City consisted of easy and relaxed banter. She felt a natural ease when she was by his side. He looked amazing in his black leather jacket. The color matched his stylish Jeep perfectly. Once they reached their destination, Luke pulled into a small lot adjacent to his restaurant and bar, "The Watering Trough". It consisted of a two story, brick building set back from the main road of the town. The street was dotted with speciality and souvenir stores. Cosette even spotted a number of ads for the famous ghost tours. They entered the quaint, candle lit establishment. Luke ushered them to a dimly lit booth in one of the far, secluded corners.

"How bout a couple of Long Island Iced teas? Those are one of our specialities," suggested Luke.

"Sounds great but only if you have one too?"

"You got yourself a deal," as he winked and confidently walked over to the sturdy wooden bar complete with rattle snake decorations and neon, flashing cactus string lights. He came back to their booth within minutes. Luke raised the generous, tall glass, "To a new and wonderful friendship." They clinked their glasses and indulged in the incredible taste of the potent cocktail.

"How has this not won any awards?" asked Cosette sincerely.

"It actually has. In 2019, we received the award for the number one best bar drinks in all of Storey County."

"Well, I'm certainly not surprised."

The duo toasted a second time and they both felt giddy with each other's company. The drink was doing its magic on Cosette. She felt relaxed and happy. The conversation became deeper and more personal. They spoke about their childhoods, their future goals, places they had visited and details about each of their families. Only Cosette's husband had been omitted from the conversation. She felt waves of guilt for not telling Luke her marital status. She self soothed and reminded herself that there was still plenty of time to divulge this inconvenient detail. The truth is, Cosette had basically no communication with Chad at this point. If there was any communication, it was strictly over text and it only revolved around their son. They had officially filed. They would be legally divorced in six months. Her goal was to get settled in Reno and then bring her son to live with her there. She had already started researching which elementary schools were the highest rated in the area. Commuting to Seattle had become close to impossible since she often only had a single day off, too short of a time span to travel back and forth. Chad was willing to let Cosette have their son full time. He only requested to have him for a few weeks during the summer.

While Cosette was in the midst of her deep thoughts, she didn't notice a curvy, sexy redhead slinking over to their table. While she had a much different look than Cosette, she was definitely the type who could be considered a man eater by most people's standards. She was voluptuous, overly confident and almost vulgar. Her blue eyes rivaled the color of the waters off of the Maldives. She was much more petite than Cosette, standing at 5'5. Her silky, strawberry mane hit just around her bare shoulders.

"Hey, Luke!" She beamed at him.

"Well, hello there, Amber. Having a busy day? How was the lunch rush?"

"We have been steady. Lots of our regulars and some tourists. Who do we have here?" She gazed critically at Cosette, clearly irked by her proximity to Luke.Luke, not missing a beat said,

"This is a good friend of mine, Cosette."Amber's gum chewing and foot tapping became audibly louder.

"Ok, whatever, do you two want an early dinner? Or what?" she hissed. Cosette ordered the Caesar salad and Luke ordered the pork chops. After the scrumptious meal, the duo took a walk down the main street of the town. They strolled past antique stores, fudge and ice cream shops, mercantile stores and a number of other watering holes and restaurants. Luke was a perfect gentleman. At one point, Cosette almost tripped on a wooden plank. Luke quickly came to her rescue and made sure that she was not injured in any way. The late afternoon sun cast long shadows on the ground before them. Soon after, the sky was ablaze with the fire of the setting sun over the dusty Nevada desert. Their conversations were natural flowing and contained a warmth similar to the tone of lifelong friends. They sat along the sidewalk and people watched. Luke seemed familiar with a large portion of the fellow street dwellers. Many of them were acquaintances and some were even friends from his childhood. At this point, it was past 9:00 p.m. The sky was inky and the air was brittle cold. Luke took off his jacket and wrapped Cosette snuggly into it. Her shivers quickly came to a halt. Cosette was so immersed in their time together and she relished every minute with him that she actually lost track of time.

"Oh no, Luke. I didn't realize that it is so late already. I have a 5:00 a.m. check in tomorrow. I am working a three day trip."

"That is too bad. Is there any way that I could get you to come visit me here again, after your trip?"

"I would love that. Would Monday work for you?"

"Monday is as perfect as it gets, Cosette. Can I pick you up in the afternoon?"

"Fantastic, I can't wait."

Luke drove her back to her hotel. To Cosette's relief, Maggie was there. She hung on to every last detail which Cosette told her. They then went to sleep in preparation for the next day's work.

7

Luke remained in the front and center of every one of Cosette's thoughts during her three day trip. She continually reminded herself that she was still a married woman and she had no business fawning over another man. Her mother always warned her that this type of behavior was the perfect recipe for a disaster. Cosette also decided that it was overdue to tell Luke that she did, indeed, still have a husband. Although his behavior towards her had, so far, been nothing but friend like, she felt it would be deceiving not to disclose her marital status to him, at this point. She could see him potentially becoming a long term, platonic friend. True friends obviously should be aware whether members of their inner circle were married or not. This knowledge was part of a normal and healthy friendship.

Cosette worked in Economy Class during her three day trip. She became fast friends with two of her flying partners, Raven and Tenley. Both had worked for World Connect Airlines for at least five years and they each shared strong ties to Virginia City themselves. Raven was born and raised there. She was an ebony haired beauty with eyes of a pale violet shade. Tenley could be described as more of a tomboy. Cute, short, honey streaked hair, light brown eyes and eye brows which did not seem to frame her face quite right. However, what she lacked in beauty, she made up for in humor and kindness. The three flight attendants enjoyed their flights and layovers together immensely.

In San Antonia, they visited a trendy bar along the river walk. The music was blasting and there was distinct electricity in the air. Tenley told Cosette that she worked at a year round Christmas decoration shop in Virginia City. She only worked as a flight attendant about six days a month. Her flying schedule allowed her to have plenty of time to dedicate to the store and live full time in her beloved Virginia City. Raven chimed in,

"I live in Virginia City too. I work at a bar on my days off." That caught Cosette's attention immediately!

"Oh, which bar?"

"The Watering Trough, it's a fun place. You should come by some time."

"I actually had dinner there on my last day off," proclaimed Cosette. Both of her flying partners' interests were instantly piqued.

"How random," exclaimed Raven. "What brought you there?"

"I have a new friend named Luke. He is the owner. He was kind enough to show me around your beautiful town." Tenley and Raven's faces turned ghost white. There was a hushed silence. Cosette's face blushed and she could feel heat rising within her.

"Is there a problem?" she asked her flying partners. They both quickly composed themselves and said,

"Absolutely not. Luke is a great man but he is known to be quite the heartbreaker." Cosette felt anxious when she heard this but she was quickly able to mask her concern.

"Well, he is just a kind friend to me."

The flight was over and Cosette was finally back at her base. She took the shuttle van to her hotel and was happy to see Maggie there. Uncharacteristically, Maggie's mood was very foul.

"What's going on?" asked Cosette concerned.

"The darn flight attendants in the room next to us have been blasting their awful music all night. I called the front desk twice and they aren't doing a thing about it." Cosette responded,

"This is starting to become a regular occurrence. They have been doing it ever since they moved in. We can't afford to keep losing sleep. Our shifts are way too long and taxing for this nonsense." They both retreated to their beds with ear plugs in place and pillows over their heads. The ruckus continued throughout the night but, It wasn't enough to dampen Cosette's mood. It was 9:00 a.m. Luke would be here later today. Her pulse quickened. She felt like a love struck teenage girl.

8

The characteristic, assertive knock boomed. Cosette quickly tousled her hair and darted to the door.

"You have got to be the most timely person I've ever known, Luke."

"Well, I am 100% Swiss, he laughed good-naturedly. I am every bit as
timely as the Swiss trains."

"It's certainly a good trait to have, added Cosette. I am part Swiss too but not completely. I have plenty of Czech coursing through my veins too." They both laughed and started on their day's adventure. They hopped into the Jeep and headed straight to Virginia City.

"I hope you are hungry because I have a little get together set up at my restaurant with a handful of my closest friends." Cosette couldn't help but feel anxious.

"Meeting a number of his friends? Talk about putting the pressure on." The restaurant was lively and packed. A group of young adults were huddled together at a table by the window. They immediately spotted Luke and Cosette and motioned them over.

"Well, this must be Cosette?" boomed one of the gentlemen in the group. Luke responded,

"It sure is. Allow me to make introductions. This is Austin Jolin. We have been close friends since kindergarten." Cosette shook his hand and was somewhat stunned by his over firm grip. He was an average looking man, stout and very muscular. He had the beginning of a receding hairline. His eyes were tired looking and they were a lack luster grey in color. He sported a complete sleeve tattoo on one arm. His fiancee, Lucy, had sparkling hazel eyes and a blunt, sun streaked bob cut. She had her arm firmly wrapped around his mid section. She gave the impression of being very protective of him. The introductions continued. "This is my cousin, Wyatt." He was a tall and muscular man. Chiseled features, razor sharp, almost harsh, cheek bones, generous lips, thick, onyx colored hair and his black eyes appeared to be impenetrable. "We didn't go to school together because he is eight years older than me but we are still best buddies. You'll see him all over town, especially in the graveyard" The entire group laughed and Cosette was not clear why that statement amused the friends.

"He is the caretaker at the cemetery," explained Luke. "He is married to his job. You will see him there day and night. He is quite a sight when he is there on nights with full moons. He has scared his share of tourists. In fact, Wyatt may be part of the reason our town has a reputation for being haunted."

There were five other men and three ladies still to be introduced to Cosette. They were all welcoming They clearly adored Luke and saw him as their idol and leader. They enjoyed a delicious and high energy, late afternoon lunch together. The drinks were poured endlessly. Amber made a point of leaning over the table while pouring the cocktails, displaying ample cleavage. Anyone with a pulse could see her finer assets. At one point, she spilled part of a drink directly onto Cosette's lap. Luke jumped up, clearly feeling mortified, and swiftly went to get some absorbent towels. Amber stated, "Gee, I'm so sorry that happened. I don't usually spill." She discreetly winked at Cosette as a clear message to her that this "accident" was in actuality intentional.

9

After the get together, Luke linked his arm through Cosette's and they went out onto the main road. A blanket of stars from above illuminated their way along the otherwise dimly lit road.

"I just realized that I still have not shown you my house. Would you like to go there and we can have a cocktail?" Masking any slight reservation, Cosette said that she would be delighted to see his home. They drove together up to a hill top within five minutes of the Watering Trough Restaurant. They pulled into the long, windy driveway. There were no other homes in the vicinity. Luke escorted her into the impressive home. Cosette was startled by what she saw. It was a very modern home. All of the windows went from floor to high ceilings. The view of the little town below was dazzling. The twinkling lights of the Virginia City homes mesmerized her. A hot tub was nestled on the large deck, jutting out just shy of the edge of the cliff. The stately home was secluded among a grouping of redwood trees. Below the deck, there were eight acres of pure magic. Cosette spotted a lush pond, a pasture and orange trees overloaded with the succulent fruit. To the left of the pasture, Cosette noticed a moon drenched, kidney-shaped pool. A three foot wide waterfall cascaded into the deep end leaving a foamy residue floating on top of the turquoise water. There was even a beach entry into the pool which gently sloped up to meet the land. The only pool toy in sight was a giant, inflatable pizza slice pool float. This put a smile on Cosette's face. She had already surmised during the brief time which she had become acquainted with Luke, that he truly enjoyed food, although his perfect physique would never hint that he was a foodie.

They sat down on an overstuffed and comfortable, white leather sofa. Luke poured each of them a top shelf flute of champagne. At first, their conversation remained superficial. They spoke about his friends and the get together they had just attended together. The champagne continued to flow generously. Shortly after, Luke asked Cosette if she recalled the girl, Eden, from the party earlier. Without saying so, Cosette thought,

"She'd be hard not to notice. She had an enviable hour glass shape, perfectly coiffed flaxen hair, teal colored, almond shaped eyes, and her eyelashes were so thick, black and long they appeared to extend into the next zip code. She was a true vixen." Instead, Cosette's response was, "Yes, I think I remember her. Was she sitting next to Wyatt?"

"Yes, exactly. Well, Eden and I have quite a past." Jealousy erupted within Cosette.

"Oh? I wasn't aware of that."

"Yeah, we started dating at the end of high school. We dated for four years. We even got engaged!"

"Wow, what happened?"

"It was a tough decision for me to make but, to this day, I know it was the right decision. I always adored her as a friend. We clicked on almost every level. In fact, we even got along with each other's families... But, I never felt a romantic love for her. I felt that what we had was enough to make a happy and successful marriage but, in time, I couldn't ignore my inner voice any longer. I wanted my wife to be my best friend, my universe and I longed to feel deeply in love with her. Unfortunately, Eden did not fit all of those qualifications. It was a very rough break up. In time, we were able to become friends again. So, that is a little about my past. Have you been in any serious relationships? You have a son, so I'm assuming there are some exes out there." This was the moment of truth. Up to this point, it was borderline deceptive not to mention her husband. After this, not disclosing that very important fact would be considered full blown lying. Chills went up and down her spine. It was now or never.

"Yes, Spencer's dad is still around……. In fact, he is my husband. We are in the process of divorcing now." Luke couldn't disguise his audible gasp and clear feelings of disappointment.

"Wow, I was not aware of that. You have never mentioned him before. Where does he live? Is he taking care of Spencer in Seattle?"

"Yes, he is." Cosette was holding back tears. "We have been married for almost five years. We were actually having a casual relationship when I discovered that I was pregnant. We felt that we needed to get married at that point, to do the right thing."

"Are you still in love with him?" Cosette responded,

"Sadly, I never have been in love with him and I never will be. It was not the way I envisioned my future marriage when I was a young girl. But, I love my son with all my heart and I would do anything to give him a happy and stable life." Luke seemed to relax after hearing more details of Cosette's marriage. He then stated,

"Here is to new beginnings. "Let's toast, to good friends." They clinked their glasses together. "We can help support each other and serve as a sounding board about future partners we might bring along," added Luke. Thankfully, for Cosette, the subject changed. They started discussing Cosette's living situation at the hotel. Cosette told Luke that she felt lucky if she could get just two hours of shut eye a night. The neighbors were incessantly rude and loud. It made it very hard to get up after such interrupted sleep and work ten plus hour shifts. That gave Luke an idea,

"Hey, I just thought of something. I have a cute, vacant, two bedroom cottage on the west-side of town. It is away from all the bar and restaurant commotion. It's on a quiet street. I'll make you a deal. Why don't you and Maggie move there and In exchange, maybe a couple of days a month, you could help out at the Watering Trough for just a few hours? Plus the cottage is only a thirty minute drive to the airport. I have an extra car that you and Maggie could share as your commuter car since your car is back in Seattle. I think you'd really like it." Cosette was overwhelmed by Luke's generosity and knew it would be an incredible help for both her and Maggie. Cosette thanked him profusely and asked if she could give him the answer tomorrow after she bounced the idea off of Maggie. Luke, of course, understood that it was critical to talk to Maggie about the offer first before accepting it.

10

Luke drove Cosette back to her hotel and returned to his town. He felt a deep sadness and yearning. Luke had only known Cosette for a short period of time but he had never once felt such an intense and immediate connection to a woman. It took every ounce of will power for him not to hold her close or entwine his fingers with hers during their outings. His every thought had been consumed by her. It scared him a great deal and it made him feel vulnerable. He wasn't generally like this. In fact, in town, he was known to be somewhat of a ladies' man. He always treated women well but refrained from committing to them. Cosette had cast a huge spell over him and, of course, she just had to be still legally married! How awful for him. He had been searching for this incredible woman his entire life. He felt a sickly pain in the pit of his stomach. He vowed to himself right then and there that, out of respect for her, he would keep his deep feelings for her a secret and commit to supporting her as a friend going through a turbulent marriage and a difficult divorce. Knowing that was the right thing to do and actually wanting to keep Cosette at the friendship level were two entirely different things. Feeling somber, he continued to drive deeper into the night towards his home.

Maggie's enthusiasm to move to the cottage in Virginia City was palpable. Her excited, broad grin and wide eyes amused Cosette. Her excitement was no less than the excitement dieters feel who finally achieve their goal weight.

"Then it's a done deal. I'll call Luke and we will get an action plan started," said Cosette.Cosette dialed Luke's number and he answered on the first ring.

"Hi there, Luke. I want to thank you again for our terrific outing yesterday. It was unforgettable."

"The pleasure was all mine. I'm glad you enjoyed it."

"Listen, Maggie and I talked and, if it is still an option, we would love to take you up on your offer and move into the cottage."

"You just made my day. The offer is very much still open. So, when is your next day off?"

"I am off from next Monday until Wednesday.

"That's ideal. I can come pick you and Maggie up with my extended pick up truck. There should be plenty of room for your clothes and luggage. I can get there on Monday morning if that works for you. That will give us a nice early start to get you both settled in."

"I'll be counting the days and thank you again so much," chimed Cosette. Once the call disconnected, Cosette felt the overwhelming urge to dance tingling in her toes. Assuming the new living accommodations were a hit, Cosette would soon bring her precious son to live with her. Maggie could sleep in one room and Cosette and Spencer could be in the other bedroom.

"Was it possible?" Cosette hesitated to jinx anything and get her hopes up but could things really be starting to fall into place?

Cosette and Maggie packed the few suitcases they had. They were not sad to leave this noise riddled hotel. Arianna Grande concerts were quieter than their current residence. Luke arrived promptly He looked more handsome than ever. His brown suede jacket emphasized his Titan style shoulders. His jeans fit him precisely and made him appear even more rugged than usual. His enthusiasm was infectious and very appealing. Being a top notch gentleman, he insisted on transporting the majority of the items down to his truck himself. Once their hotel room was vacant, the three of them hopped into the truck and never looked back. It was a residence they would not soon miss.

Shortly after entering Virginia City's town limits, Luke veered sharply to the right and continued along a dusty road. Within a minute of driving, a vintage cottage came into sight. It crouched low into the daisy filled meadow. A sequence of large, slate grey rocks created a walkway up to the front door. The paneled and wooden door was a fitting piece to round out the welcoming cottage. In fact, it almost beckoned its visitors to enter. Past the lawn area, the desert sand encircled the property. The cottage had a fairytale like appearance. The home was situated on one level and it was made solely of dark red bricks. Hedges and honeysuckles provided the cottage with additional privacy. The closest neighbors were at least a five minute walk away. The trio walked up the slightly rickety three steps to the front door.Luke proclaimed,

"Here goes." He unlocked the front door and they entered into a large main room complete with a sofa and two wooden rocking chairs. Antique lamps were displayed on the three delicate glass end tables. Luke quickly illuminated the room. There were large windows throughout the room. The room became submerged in light. Cosette immediately fell in love with the cottage. They proceeded to walk down a short hallway and entered the homey kitchen. Luke proudly commented,

"My father made this entire cottage with his bare hands." Cosette and Maggie gasped and expressed their deep admiration. The walls of the kitchen were a glossy, mood lifting, sunlit yellow. The appliances were fairly new and they were all stark white in color. There was ample cupboard and counter space. Dishes, a microwave, a toaster, utensils and even an electric wine opener were all included with the cottage. Next, they went to tour the two bedrooms and two baths. One of the bedrooms had a magnificent view of the desert. The town's graveyard could be seen just a short distance away. The other bedroom overlooked a courtyard. Lush plants, a koi pond and even a resin, cascading, tiered fountain bubbled quietly. Both ladies were speechless and overjoyed.

"You ladies have had a long day. Why don't I leave you to get settled. I will be sure to check in tomorrow but if you need anything at all in the meantime, please text or call me." Cosette and Maggie thanked Luke for his kindness.After he left, they both collapsed wearily onto the sofa. Their bones ached. Cosette unsuccessfully tried to suppress a yawn. Soon after, Cosette whipped up an easy meal for them, spaghetti with meat sauce and a side salad. They enjoyed a tasty Merlot during dinner. As it got closer to bedtime, it was time to discuss which bedroom each lady would get. Maggie, never one to hold back or have a filter, asked to have the room with the koi pond view. "I would rather not sleep in the other room. Graveyards just freak me out". Cosette was too weary to argue. They both went to their separate bedrooms and fell asleep the moment their heads hit the pillows.

11

The soft rays of sunlight danced on Cosette's face in the morning. It took her a moment to orient herself and realize that she was all snug and toasty in her new, cozy cottage in none other than Virginia City. She stretched lazily, like a Persian cat disturbed from a deep slumber. She walked over to her window and was blown away by the view. The desert sand was already starting to bake despite the early morning hour. From the corner of her eye she sensed a quick movement. She looked over and saw a roadrunner bird rapidly crossing in the shaded area on the left side of the backyard. He mingled amongst the scattered brush and repeatedly called out, "Coo". He then settled into what could only be described as a morning sunbathing routine. He lay in a sun drenched area of the yard and raised his feathers. By doing this, it was evident that the rays were able to reach his skin. Perhaps, he was warming himself after enduring a frigid desert night? After this, he ran swiftly to the bird bath and began to drink copious amounts of water. Cosette enjoyed watching his antics. She hoped he would become a regular visitor. Her thoughts were interrupted by the ping of her phone. It was exactly who she was hoping to hear from, Luke!

"Good morning, sunshine. I hope the bed was comfy? Did you sleep well?"

"I sure did. That was probably the best sleep I've had in years. Now I get the pleasure of admiring my new friend, a beautiful roadrunner."

"That's wonderful to hear. You'll be seeing a lot more of those scoundrels. Hey, I'm having a barbecue and swim party tonight at my house. Any chance that I could entice you to join us?"

The Stalker in the Desert

"I'd love that. Would it be ok if I brought Maggie too?" Cosette sensed the slightest of hesitation before Luke enthusiastically said,

"Yes, of course. The party starts at 5:00 p.m. The pool is solar heated to 93 degrees and I will have outdoor heaters so I think it will make for a pretty comfortable night."Cosette told Maggie all of the party details over breakfast. Maggie's face beamed like a child who had just won a stuffed animal at the carnival. Maggie looked pensive suddenly as she gently bit her lower lip. "So, a swim party?" We need to figure out stat which suits we are going to wear." Cosette said that she wasn't too concerned since she only had two suits to choose from.The girls wore their favorite bikinis and stylish swim cover ups. Both had perfectly made manicures and pedicures.Their nails looked brightly colored and glossy. Cosette's toes were a vibrant red, Maggie's were a dark fuchsia.

They drove up to Luke's home, on the hill. Maggie was speechless, which was unusual for her.

"This isn't a house! It's more like a mansion! Sweet Jesus!" Several cars were already parked along the quarter mile long driveway. Cosette gently parked her borrowed, sky blue Toyota Camry into a spot and the ladies proceeded to the front door. The door was already wide open. A DJ was playing all of the latest hits. A staff member guided the ladies down to the pool area. Maggie had a hard time keeping her jaw from dropping. She whispered to Cosette,

"What opulence. What wealth!"

Luke was surrounded by at least a dozen of his friends next to the poolside bar. The moment Cosette stepped onto the pool deck, Luke became completely distracted with his ongoing conversations and stared longingly at Cosette. That woman unnerved him like nobody ever had.He quickly approached them, welcomed them to the gathering and hugged both ladies. Maggie's hold on him seemed to linger uncomfortably long but he chalked her actions up to being an anxious new girl in town.The girls were served cocktails and they engaged in conversation with Luke. Eden, his ex girlfriend, was glued to his side. Some of the party goers jumped into the steaming, turquoise pool water. Luke said,

"Shall we take a dip?" The girls eagerly agreed. Maggie and Cosette removed their swim covers and jumped directly into the deepest part of the pool. Luke was in a playful mood and splashed Cosette. Her face was completely baptized by the pool water. She laughed heartily and exclaimed,

"That's it, you little brat." She dove under the water and high tailed directly to Luke's submerged feet and tickled him. An all out mini war started. Their chemistry was evident to all. Maggie was left in the shadows sulking. Luckily, nobody noticed the bitter scowl forming on her face. The high jinks continued for about another hour and then the guests ascended from the pool and sat around a number of patio tables. The outdoor heaters were doing their magic. They made the backyard oasis feel like a balmy July evening. Of course, Luke made absolutely sure to grab the seat next to Cosette. Maggie was seated on Cosette's other side. They continued sipping their made to order cocktails. All of a sudden, Maggie excused herself from the table indicating that she needed to visit the powder room. Luke and Cosette were so engrossed in their conversation that they did not even notice her departure.

12

Maggie went into the house at a rapid speed.
"As I entered the house at the beginning of
the party, I noticed a line of keys latched to key
holders in the far end of the entry hall. I knew
seeing those keys would help me to eventually
concoct a plan." She went directly to the glittering
keys and sifted thought them. She found a key to
Luke's Lamborghini, alongside one for his
restaurant, and one labeled, "Mom".

Her nerves became increasingly frazzled. She
cautiously looked around in hopes of not seeing
any of the other party goers in the vicinity. All

was clear. She delved deeper into his extensive key collection.

"At last, there it was. Not just one house key but four of them. I highly doubt he will notice if one is missing," she giggled to herself feeling utterly self satisfied. She slipped the key into a zipped side pouch of her handbag. "And the first part of my mission is accomplished." She strutted confidently back to her table and commenced with the obligatory small talk.

Cosette and Maggie were the last two guests remaining at the party. They thanked Luke for a beautiful evening and returned home to their cottage. Maggie was unusually quiet, almost stone faced, in the car. It was unlike her. She was Cosette's best friend and her warmth and enthusiasm always made their friendship even closer.

"Is everything ok, Maggie?"

"Oh, absolutely. I am just so tired. I am relieved I have some more days off,"Cosette chimed in,

"I wish I did. I have a three day trip starting tomorrow."

"I am sure you will have fun on your trip though," Maggie stated flatly and unenthusiastically.

Cosette left at five in the morning the following day for her early check in at the airport. Maggie felt a huge sense of relief when she woke up closer to 9:00 a.m. and realized that her "bestie" was long gone. It was time to start putting her plan into action. It was critical that her scheme would get orchestrated without a hitch. She listened intently to the conversations she overheard Luke having at the party the night before. All of a sudden, she startled and remembered a critical detail. Luke asked his cousin, Wyatt, and two other friends to meet him after his work shift at 10:00 tonight. He said they could have drinks and shoot pool. Tonight was the night to put her master plan into action. She smiled mischievously and felt relieved that her scheme was becoming more thought out and imminent.

Evening could not arrive quickly enough for Maggie. She went into town and got a spray tan and then she went to a nail salon and got the sexiest acrylic nails she had ever seen.

"These Virginia City people sure know their business. They are friendly and very skilled at their jobs." At around 9:00 p.m., she let herself into Luke's palatial home. She did not feel an ounce of guilt. She truly believed that they were meant to be together. Now. if she could just get Luke's mind off of Cosette.

"I'd be as good as engaged if I could get him to forget about her. He needs a real woman, not a little, do-gooder of a girl. I would always keep our relationship exciting. I would leave him constantly wanting for more and tonight, I will prove this to him."

13

She found her way to his bedroom. She was not disappointed by what she saw. The room was enormous, opulent and sensual. It was luxurious and high ceilinged, presidential even. One entire wall consisted of a large window. The fog crept in slow motion towards the window, almost in a mirage like and mysterious way. It crawled over the hedges noiselessly and then, within minutes, the spooky, grey entity enveloped the window and shrouded the glorious views Maggie had enjoyed seeing just moments before.The walls were decked with desert themed paintings, a coyote lonesomely howling off in the distant mountains and a field overflowing with striking desert flowers.She sauntered over to his dresser. The few photos he had on display gave few clues to his life. He had a gold framed portrait of his parents. His father was also a striking, dark haired gentleman. They looked very similar. His mother reminded her of a Barbie doll. The cliche of perfect, yet unrealistic measurements, peroxide blonde hair and piercing blue eyes.

"His mom definitely had visited the plastic surgeon on more than one occasion." His bed was king-size, overstuffed with several pillows and very masculine print sheets were adorned in velvet. Maggie felt a flash of anger and jealousy.

"How many women had he entertained in this love chamber of his?"

She took a few deep breaths to calm herself down. Jealousy and anxiety would only thwart her efforts at this point. Soon enough, every woman from his past would be nothing but a faded, negative memory and she would take the rightful and well deserved title of queen of his heart and soul." On Luke's nightstand, Maggie spotted a sparkling crystal decanter filled with a rich, amber liquid.

"Well, if I've ever needed liquid courage, it would be about now." She uncapped the high end container and drank directly from it. She took several gulps. The potent liquid seared her throat with its intensity. The digital clock on Luke's other nightstand indicated it was already 10:39 p.m.

"Let's see, his restaurant closed at 10:00 p.m. He would still drink and shoot pool with a few friends. If Luke was home by midnight, I would be lucky," she thought glumly. She lay on his bed and tried to relax and, once again, go over her exact game plan. She imagined the outcome would be everything she had ever dreamed of. By the time she left Luke, hopefully after breakfast tomorrow morning, she would be his and he would be hers. "Now and forever." She sighed, feeling elated and satisfied with the thought.

Midnight came and went. Maggie grew increasingly anxious and impatient. Finally, shortly after 1:00 a.m., she heard the front door unlatch. It was finally the moment of truth. She was wearing sky scraper high, stiletto heels and a white, laced teddy. Fortunately, she had just touched up her makeup and combed her hair moments before his arrival. She could hear Luke in the kitchen. The fridge opened and closed and so did several drawers. She heard the microwave spring to life. "Seriously, I am here in the bedroom waiting for him and he is taking his time heating up corn dogs? Men!"

About another ten minutes passed. Then it happened. He was approaching! Maggie could hear his heavy footsteps plodding towards the master bedroom. The lighting in the room cast a soft, pink glow. She had even lit a few candles which encircled the bed. Luke entered the room and looked as if he was on the verge of screaming out in pure terror. His skin turned as white as the pale moon outside. Instead of the warm welcome Maggie expected, Luke boomed,

"Maggie, what the hell are you doing here, and how did you get into my house?"

"You see a beautiful woman on your bed and that's your biggest concern?" Luke, remembering that Maggie was Cosette's best friend, softened his tone.

"I am sorry. I'm just a little confused as to why you are in my house?"

"Isn't it obvious, big boy?" Luke's face tuned every possible shade of red. "I don't bite. Come over here and sit next to me." Luke cautiously went over to her. "Luke, I am going to lay it on the line. I'm not a game player. We are both young, both single, both beautiful. I've seen how you look at me. Heck, it borders on leering." At this, Maggie laughed at her own joke. Luke was mortified that he had unintentionally given her this idea. In fact, nothing could be further from the truth but he knew that handling this very uncomfortable situation with kindness and grace was crucial.

"Wow, Maggie. I am so flattered. You are a wonderful woman. Any guy would be lucky to have you."

"I don't want any guy. I want you," she retorted sharply. At that, she reached out and pulled him close to her, planting a soft, deep kiss on his mouth." Luke acted as if he had been electrocuted. He recoiled and could not even bother to mask his utter disgust. Maggie's face became distorted and the look in her eyes bordered on insanity.

"Oh, I know what this is about. You want my best friend. You are a fool. She is a married woman and she has a son, for God's sake."Luke was speechless. Wanting Cosette was an understatement. He had grown deeply in love with her. In fact, she was the only woman he had ever truly loved.

Maggie was not in the mood for further conversation. She jumped up in a fitful rage, threw on her London Fog coat and stormed out of the house. Maggie did not drive to Luke's house for fear that he would spot her car when he returned home. At least she had enough foresight to pack an extra pair of high top Converse shoes. She began her trek back to the cottage, feeling utterly humiliated, jealous, even livid.She gazed at the night sky which seemed to stretch to infinity. The faraway howls of coyotes broke the silence of the night. Maggie felt terrified and melancholic. The air was icy and the tree lined path made her surroundings even darker and more eerie. She wiped the sweat from her brow. Due to the fog, her visibility was greatly obscured. She was barely able to see three feet in front of her. It reminded her of a movie she had once seen about the living dead. The ground beneath her was soggy due to the droplets from the fog. Her high tops felt glued into the soft earth. A thunderous noise boomed above.

"Thunder! Of course. What else could go wrong?" The tree trunks seemed to press in on her from all sides. Soon there were hints of light in the distance. After about a hundred more steps, Maggie exited the forested trail. At last, she was in town. The street were deserted, but at least some street lights helped to illuminate her way. She saw the graveyard in the near distance. With a huge sigh of relief, she realized that once she reached the graveyard, the cottage would arrive shortly after.

Maggie decided to go through the graveyard since it was more brightly lit than the surrounding shrubbery. She walked at an increasingly hurried pace. Suddenly, she crashed into a tall man. They both gasped. To her relief, she recognized that he was Luke's cousin.

" Hello, little lady. Why on earth are you walking through a cemetery in the middle of the night?" Maggie defensively responded,

"Well, why are you here?" He laughed heartily and retorted,

"I work here. Remember? You don't look like you're doing too well, Maggie? Is everything ok?"

"Sure, I will be fine." Wyatt was far from convinced.

"Here, have a Heineken." Maggie snorted and laughed despite herself.

"You have beer in the graveyard?"

"Darn right I do and a lot of it. It gets lonely to be here all night, every night. I need something to help me pass the time." Maggie agreed with his statement and they sat on a bench together. Maggie could spot a perfect view of Cosette's darkened window from this location. They started to talk about a multitude of subjects, childhood pets, favorite books, their mutual love of water skiing and snowmobiling. As friends, they seemed to click very well. Wyatt prodded again,

"Now, ya want to tell me what had you so upset? I've been told I'm a good listener and the only people I tell secrets to are the inhabitants of my cemetery."At that, they both chuckled. It took little convincing for Maggie to spill every last detail to her new friend. Wyatt pondered Maggie's dilemma and then after some thoughtful consideration said,

"I know exactly what's going on. If you ask me, my cousin is head over heels in love with Cosette. Hell, he'd never admit it to me but I can see it when he looks at her. He has never even come close to acting like this with any other woman. Not even hot, little Eden and he was actually engaged to her."

This is exactly what Maggie had suspected. Maggie exclaimed,

"But it's laughable. She's a married woman and she even has a kid."

"You love who you love, I guess. Doesn't mean he will act on it. If I know my cousin, he will pine away for her for a lifetime but never admit his feelings to her out of respect for her marriage." Maggie began to tear up. She was starting to resent, maybe even hate her so called best friend. Tears rolled down her cheeks.

Wyatt's thoughts included things nobody could ever possibly even guess. He had developed a full, all consuming, obsession for the enticing Cosette himself. He spent large parts of his night shift at the cemetery trying to watch Cosette through her bedroom window. His binoculars came in very handy for his sightings. He wanted Cosette. He needed her. He couldn't care less that she was married. Unlike his goody two shoes cousin, he was ruthless. He wanted to own her, to consume her, to make her his wife and once they got married, he'd never let her out of his sight again. What infuriated and scared him the most was that he noticed that Cosette often looked at his cousin sideways, somewhat flirty and enamored. He wouldn't let anything develop between them. If it was the last thing he did, he would keep them apart and make her his! Maybe this pathetic girl next to him could work with him to make both of their dreams come true.

14

The next morning, Wyatt texted Maggie, "We need to talk. Could you meet me at the cemetery tonight at ten?" Maggie was intrigued and quickly responded that she would be there.

"Have my beer ready and chilled! I will be there!" They met up at exactly 10:00 p.m. at the same bench as where they sat the previous evening.

"You definitely piqued my curiosity. What's going, Wyatt?"

"Can I trust you?"

"Of course you can, silly."

"Ok, here goes. Let's cut to the chase. I know how smitten you are with Luke." Maggie corrected him,

"I'm not smitten. I am truly in love with him."

"Ok, whatever, I know how you can get him!" Maggie had goosebumps on top of goosebumps after his statement.

"Go on…I'm listening."

"It's simple. I think Cosette has the hots for Luke too. If you tell her things about him to disgust her, she will lose interest in him. Then she will stop spending time with him and she will probably act colder with him. Her frigid behavior will then turn Luke off. He will get over her and voila, he will see that you are the best choice for him after all. You will be a shoulder for him to cry on and a loyal, patient friend. You'll have it in the bag. I promise this will work. She gets home from her trip tomorrow, Right? This is what you'll need to tell her…"

The two conspired and planned for at least another hour. Then they both went their separate ways, feeling confident about their plan. Both of them convinced that their scheme was going to work.

As planned, Cosette retuned from her trip two days later. She was yearning to get to her cottage. It felt like home for her. She had been communicating with Chad in the last week and he had agreed to let Spencer move to Virginia City to be with her full time. It was not like him to make anything easy for his estranged wife. To say she was elated, would be a huge understatement. She needed her son like a heart needs a beat. If there were no delays with paperwork, he would be moving to be with her in just nineteen and a half days. But, who was counting?" she thought with a smile. In fact, she had already hired a University of Nevada student, Robin, to be his nanny when Cosette had to go away on trips. She was counting the minutes to show Spencer all around town. The most exciting part for her was to introduce him to Romeo, her regular roadrunner visitor. Spencer would share a room with Cosette, so he would have the delight of watching the bird's antics every morning as well. Cosette had grown very fond of Romeo. She enjoyed photography a great deal. It was actually one of her deepest passions. Romeo had the honor of often being the model and center point of her projects. His portraits were displayed in a number of high profile spots in the cottage. In fact, she even referred to him as her pet when she showed the photos of him to her flying partners. He had developed quite a fan base and following among Cosette's colleagues.

Cosette was thrilled to see Maggie as she entered the front room. Maggie's eyes were puffy and she looked sleep deprived.

"Maggie, I missed you so much. How are you?"

"I'm just dandy," she retorted sarcastically. Cosette settled in next to her on the comfy sofa.

"Talk to me, Maggie"

"I swear, it is nothing. You know what we need? Two nice, tall jack and cokes!"

"Now you're speaking my language," Cosette laughed. The ladies stretched out on the reclining sofa and sipped their cocktails.

Cosette gave full details of her trip to New Orleans.

"The restaurants there are to die for. I even had beignets with extra powdered sugar at the famous, Cafe Du Monde. I took a tour of the Mardi Gras floats too. They are stored in a large warehouse. It was unforgettable." Soon both girls had downed three drinks each, and these were stiff drinks. They could practically come out of the pump at the local Chevron Station and blend in perfectly with the actual gasoline. Maggie began to embark on Wyatt's devious plan.

"Cosette, there is something bothering me. I need to talk to you. You are my best friend in the whole world. I can't trust anyone else with this."

Cosette was fully alert and concerned now.

"Of course, Maggie. You know that I'm always here for you."

"I worked at the bar last night to help Luke out. My shift was only two hours long but it felt endless. Luke made inappropriate comments about my cleavage. He continuously brushed up against me too."

Maggie pretended to be holding back tears. Cosette was crushed and in an utter state of disbelief but her first loyalty had to be to her best friend.

"Are you sure his behavior wasn't misinterpreted, Maggie?"

"Absolutely not. To tell you the truth, he kind of creeps me out." Cosette was speechless. Maggie continued, "I work there again tomorrow evening. A lot of other people will probably be around so I'm not too worried."

Cosette quickly brainstormed. "I have an airport standby shift tomorrow evening but if I don't get called out for a flight, I will be able to make it to the bar at just about the time your shift ends. Then we can make sure you get home safe and sound. Would that make you feel better?"

"That sounds perfect. You really are the best!" The friends hugged but Cosette had a horrible feeling in the pit of her stomach. The ladies each went to their separate bedrooms. As soon as Cosette was out of Maggie's sight, she went briskly into her bedroom and vaulted onto her bed. She hugged her pillow and she could feel her lungs rummaging for oxygen. The flesh under her ribcage seared. Her mind was in a jumble. She didn't know what to think about Maggie's allegations against Luke. Then she admitted something to herself. Something she had never allowed herself to admit before, even

within her own mind. She loved this man. She
really loved this man. He was everything she had
ever wanted. He had become her best friend. He
was her protector. In fact, he felt like family to
her. And when she thought of him, her mouth
went dry and her heart rate quickened. He had
embedded himself deeply into her heart and
soul. She thought she had been in love one time
before, when she was merely seventeen years
old. Now she saw that those feelings from the
past were merely puppy love. The love she felt
for Luke was the real deal. He gave her so much
joy but also a great deal of pain. She wanted to
spend eternity with him. The pain she felt came
from the possibility that they may never actually
progress beyond the friendship stage. He treated
her better than anyone ever had. He put her on a
pedestal. He was true to his word and always
showered her with the highest level of respect
and attention. His actions could simply be the
behavior of a very loyal and kind friend. To now
hear, from Maggie, that Luke was making
inappropriate comments to her was enough to
destroy her heart and her trust in him. As she
drifted into a deep sleep her last thoughts were,

"Tell me the universe wouldn't be this cruel to me. I feel that I finally found the love of my life and now it seems like my entire life could go up into a blazing inferno."

Maggie went to her room and felt a deep satisfaction. Had their conniving plan actually worked? Cosette sure looked forlorn and shaken up. Maggie couldn't help but chuckle at the thought.

"I just bet I have gotten myself one step closer to being in Luke's arms, now and forever." She fell into a deep sleep. Her dreams were filled with Luke on bended knee, begging her to be his bride. She dreamt of their honeymoon. He took her to Switzerland and introduced her to his countless cousins, aunts and uncles. They held each other all night, every night, lost in the throes of passion.

She woke up in the morning with a big smile on her face and a warm, happy heart. As she lazily pulled herself out of bed, she whispered to herself,

"Now it is time to make all the beautiful dreams I have at night turn into my reality." With that affirming and very ambitious thought, she stomped into the sunlit kitchen and started her day.

Maggie reported to her shift at the Watering Trough just a few minutes late. She was slightly delayed because she had pulled out all the stops to make herself extra irresistible to Luke this evening. Her magnetic lashes made her eyes look enormous. The teeth bleaching kit she had used just before walking to Luke's restaurant had removed any lingering coffee stains. She even lightly spritzed herself from head to toe with her expensive Cartier Perfume. Her midnight black leather mini skirt showed off her curves to perfection and her tight lace, baby blue halter top left very little to the imagination. For the final touch, she put on her sky high Louboutin heels. Most women had a difficult time walking in those type of heels. For Maggie, her red bottomed shoes were like a second skin. She walked with ease in them. Her 18K gold, initial M pendant was nestled perfectly and accentuated her double Ds. Frankly, she was at risk of causing car accidents and she knew it. She sauntered confidently into the dimly lit establishment.

Luke was busy tending to customers at the bar when he spotted Maggie. Dread twisted in his gut and his legs felt wobbly. He had been disgusted ever since Maggie had made overtures towards him the other night at his home. He felt a below zero connection to her and found her mannerisms to be off putting. What made matters worse was that he was madly in love with this woman's best friend. He felt dishonest not disclosing the incident with Maggie to Cosette. Maggie had begged him to forget that it had ever happened. In between hysterical sobs, she insisted that her friendship with Cosette would be officially over if this event was ever to be told to Cosette. Then Maggie went a step further and insisted that, at that point, her life would be over as well. She pleaded for Luke to allow her to continue working at his bar. Maggie didn't catch Luke rolling his eyes at her dramatic comments. His thoughts were,

"Talk about theatrical." Against his better judgement, Luke had not mentioned anything to Cosette, yet, and he foolishly had allowed her to continue working at the Watering Trough.

"Hey there, Luke. Sorry I'm a droplet late. I'm sure I was worth the wait," as she winked coyly at him.

"It's good to see you. I can definitely use some extra hands. We have been swamped. Amber and I have been making Rumsky drinks all night. We can't make them fast enough. Would you mind going to my buddy, Carter, at the Rusty Scupper, and asking him for as many bottles of Myer's Rum as he can possibly part with? I know it is not the most high end rum but it sure seems to keep our customers happy. His bar is only about a five minute walk. Take a left once you exit our front door. Walk until the third hanging night lantern. At that point, take a right. Now here is where it gets very dark. There aren't any street lights on that road. I'd feel better if you took my Mag Light. Once you get there, Carter will be by the front window since he is expecting you." Maggie was not thrilled with this assignment but she was not about to deny Luke's request. She had always been fearful of the dark but she wanted to act cool and calm in front of Luke.

"Okey dokie, I'll head over there now. See you in a bit."

I really appreciate this, Maggie. You are a life saver. If there are more than a few bottles, have him help you carry them back here."

"Will do. See you later."

15

Maggie slipped out into the semi darkness of the main road. Plenty of people were traversing the street. She even saw Austin, Luke's friend since kindergarten. They waved enthusiastically and smiled warmly at each other and then they continued on their separate ways. He appeared to be rushed. She finally reached the third hanging lantern. She took a right and turned onto the side street. The entire vibe in the air changed. It was pitch black. Only a few stars blinked overhead. The road changed from smooth, seamless paved cement to wooden planks. Walking in her heels on this street was much more challenging. She wobbled and her limbs began to shake uncontrollably. Before she knew it, she tripped and fell in a sudden thud onto the rough street. All at once, she heard heavy, strong footsteps. These steps had a clear purpose. She saw a large man and he was racing towards her in the most menacing way. Maggie's terror mounted with each of his approaching steps. Her heart hammered in her chest.

"Is this really how it is going to end for me?" She was paralyzed with fear and she felt weighed down by dread. The man stood over her.

"Miss, are you okay? I'm Sheriff Hopkins but please call me, Jasper." Relief washed over Maggie like a tsunami. She used Luke's Mag light and could see Jasper's kind features. His large, brown, doe like eyes comforted her and helped to calm her. She explained to him that she was heading to the Rusty Scupper to pick up some rum. Once Jasper ensured that Maggie was not injured, he reached out his strong, broad, calloused hands and helped to gently and, with great care, pull her up. You are two doors away from your destination. I will drive you there and then bring you back to Luke's restaurant. Maggie's gratitude was immeasurable. As Luke had promised, Carter was waiting with twelve bottles of Myer's Rum. Maggie thanked him profusely. Then, Jasper carried the boxes for her to his patrol car and drove Maggie back to the Watering Trough. Jasper, once again, carried the boxes directly to Luke's bar top. Luke looked concerned when he saw the sheriff entering his establishment with Maggie.

"Is everything ok? Did something happen?" Maggie explained that she had slipped on the wobbly planks and that the sheriff had graciously come to her assistance.

"You are my hero, Sheriff Jasper," Maggie beamed at him with genuine
gratitude.

"Aww shucks. That is kind of you to say. I am just happy I found you as quickly as I did. I would hate for you to have been stuck on that dark road alone at this time of night. It's a creepy road, even for me." Luke, Maggie and Jasper all laughed and heartily agreed.

"Maggie, you've been through enough for one night. Why don't you sit over there, relax and have a drink?" suggested Luke.

"I might just take you up on that tempting offer," she giggled. Maggie sat on one of the rich, buttery leather bar stools and positioned herself so she could gaze at Luke as he worked. She ordered one Long Island Iced Tea after the next. It was already past 11:00 p.m. Since it was a Tuesday night, the restaurant and bar had completely emptied out. Maggie was not about to leave Luke's side for a millisecond before closing time. They made small talk for a bit. Then he apologized and said that he needed to go out back and deal with a shipment which had arrived earlier.

"I need to count and organize the merchandise." Luke clearly meant this as a hint for Maggie to head on home. It didn't work.

"Ok, well You take your time. I'll nurse my cocktail and read a novel I picked up at the town library a few days ago."

Luke walked behind her and went out the side entrance. Maggie became engrossed in her juicy romance novel. She kept pretending that Luke and she were the in love couple in the book. She sighed and took another large gulp of her drink. The alcohol made her feel light headed and relaxed. It was a good feeling. All of a sudden, she felt firm hands on either side of her waist. The feeling was titillating. It seemed that Luke was finally coming to his senses and realized he wanted her every bit as much as she wanted him. She turned seductively around. This was going to end up being the night of her dreams after all. She glanced up and what she saw was a horrifying, menacing cloaked figure. He had the most evil glint in his beady eyes. Maggie fought a rising panic as her heart leapt into her throat.

She opened her mouth to scream but before a sound could escape, the monster swung a meat tenderizer viciously onto the center of her skull. She collapsed to the ground in a heavy thump. She felt a black liquid cover her eyes and then she was elevated above her own body looking down at the scene of horror below her. Despite the gruesome sight, she felt an overwhelming sense of peace. Her mind kept reciting "Luke, Luke, Luke." At that point, she went towards and entered the irresistible, beckoning light.

"Well, that was easy." He laughed. "Almost too easy, I prefer a little more of a struggle for my liking." Maggie's eyes were open and vacant. Her pupils were fixed and dilated. Blood dripped from her head and it was beginning to pool beneath her. Her heavily painted, almost vulgar, ruby red lips were gaping apart. Her lips were a perfect match to the crimson liquid flowing from her wound. He admired the beautiful color. He quickly rifled through her overstuffed, antique, lavender handbag and spotted her cell phone. Of course, it was password protected. He placed the phone in front of her whitening face. Since her eyes were ajar, he was able to use face recognition to access her iPhone 13 Pro. He rapidly scrolled through her contacts, never forgetting for a moment that someone could walk into the room at any moment. He found Cosette's contact and texted her.

"Hey, Cosette, I'm kind of getting freaked out. Luke is acting so suggestive. Please come to the restaurant as fast as you can." Send! He threw the phone callously onto her abdomen. In his mind, she was simply meat thrown onto the floor. Then for his final touch, (this part had always been his favorite aspect of his cherished kills) he grabbed Maggie's pricey shoes and broke the heel off. He then anchored it into her awaiting mouth. This was such a critical part to his pleasure that he even made sure that he always included a stiletto heeled shoe in his kill pack. He laughed in delight at his perfect planning and antics. He then made a dash for the exit and vanished into the night, whistling the entire time. He felt so satisfied and relieved. He had been binge watching forensic shows since he was a teenager. He was proud of his skills and his great talent of always being able to go undetected after his killings. And there had been so many killings. For years, he worked as a long haul trucker. It was the ideal career for him. He eliminated more vile lot lizards and pretty, little guests at truck stops than he could even begin to estimate. He relished the power. He was ecstatic when they begged him for mercy. The women's tears flowed and left streaks on their faces even though they had so called "waterproof" mascara on their lashes. The tears poured and left a trail down their cheeks which were covered in two inch thick layers of foundation, powder and blush.

Sadly, he eventually had no choice but to give up his trucking job and move back to Virginia City. Family business had called him home. His set location made it much more difficult to regularly perform his murders. He was too high profile. All of the residents in the town were acutely aware of everyone else's business.

16

Luke realized he had been working on his inventory much longer than expected. He felt a little rude to leave Maggie deserted like that. He entered the restaurant and did not see Maggie sitting on the bar stool.

"Hmmm, she must have gone home." He walked towards the bar and saw Maggie collapsed on the floor. His immediate thought was that she must have tripped again because of her stilettos. As he went closer to her, a scene of horror played out before him. He could see blood coagulating around her.

"Oh my god! Maggie? What the hell is going on?" He bent down to her and saw her face with wide open eyes staring absently at him. He tried to wail but terror sealed his throat. He felt like he might vomit. Of course, he, in vain, checked for a pulse. He didn't detect one. He called 911 as his stomach cramped and an indescribable dread twisted in his chest.

Cosette was on her way home after finishing her standby shift at the airport. At a stoplight, she was able to check a text which had pinged a few minutes earlier. What she saw, made her head spin. It was a text from Maggie and she sounded frantic.

"Luke is acting suggestive!"

"What the heck was going on?"

As the light turned green, she put the pedal to the metal and made a dash to Luke's restaurant. The ambulance arrived moments later in a blur of lights. Sirens could be heard throughout the town. Two paramedics raced into the restaurant and went over to Maggie's lifeless body. It didn't take a neurosurgeon to see that she was deceased but only a medical examiner could officially declare death. Just minutes later, Sheriff

Jasper darted into the establishment and saw Maggie's corpse. He appeared visibly saddened and, at the same time knew, from a quick assessment, that this was clearly a homicide. Cosette was almost at her destination when she saw a great deal of commotion. She parallel parked in the first available spot and shot like a speed train into the Watering Trough. Luke was the first person she saw. His normally olive complexion was ashen. He tried to quickly comfort her and tell her what had happened but the commotion just twenty feet behind him spoke for itself.

"Maggie? Is that Maggie?" She tried to fight back a rising panic. Terror stabbed her heart and her entire body trembled. Luke tried to hold her but she was entering a complete state of panic and she became inconsolable. She collapsed to the floor and started screaming.

"What happened, Luke?" The sheriff gently told Luke and Cosette that they were not to leave the building. Jasper called in for back up. He began securing and processing the scene. He initiated a preliminary survey and took meticulous notes.

Detective Metcalf and Detective Alexander arrived at the scene. Shortly thereafter, a crime scene photographer arrived. The place was swarming with people and cameras were flashing. Luke was finally able to hold Cosette. They were collapsed in a corner booth. Both were clearly emotionally gutted and dumb founded. Cosette tried not to look over at Maggie but once when she couldn't help but look, she noticed, to her horror, that Maggie's face was starting to look increasingly like a wax figure. She darted her eyes away and vowed not to look in that direction again. There was complete silence between Luke and Cosette. She derived some comfort from feeling Luke's arms around her. She could feel his heartbeat. The excess speed of the beat further exemplified the stress and terror he was feeling. She wanted to calm him too.

Both detectives approached them. They made introductions. Detective Metcalf was soothing and had a warmth which helped to deescalate the situation a little.

"Please, call me Harper." Detective Alexander was kind but came across as much more high strung and nervous.

"Perhaps her anxiety is because she is newer in her job?" considered Cosette

"Call me Kelly, please."

Kelly requested that the duo come down to the sheriff's office for questioning. This unnerved them both. Kelly sensed their worry and quickly explained that this was just a routine follow up.

"I can drive you over there now," offered Harper. Kelly, you can stay here and continue to evaluate and make a write-up of the physical evidence." Austin entered the restaurant and walked over to them.

"What the hell is going on here?" Harper looked at Kelly and said in a brisk tone, "We really need to close off the building. I don't want any more unauthorized people entering the crime scene. In a less pleasant voice now, she demanded,

"Austin, why don't you come down with us to the station for questioning too."

"Are you kidding? This must be some kind of a joke. I was driving back from my fiancee's house and saw all the commotion in front of Luke's bar. It looks like World War III out there. Of course, I was going to come in and check on my best buddy."

"I can understand that but it is standard procedure to interview all individuals at the scene. I am sure you want the monster who did this to be brought to justice just as much as we do." With that, the trio followed the detective to her car and she rushed them to the sheriff's office.

17

They entered the nondescript building and were asked to take a seat in the waiting area. The walls were completely bare and they were a stark white shade. There were two cubicles off to one side and a few benches located along the walls, throughout the room. In the other corner stood a water cooler and a small table with a filled coffee pot. At the reception desk, sat a grouchy looking, heavy set, middle aged blonde. It was clear that she was long past the honeymoon phase of her job.

"Help yourselves to any coffee or water," she offered in an impatient tone.The three friends sat quietly in the room and then the receptionist called Luke.

"Follow me, please." Luke got up and trailed the lady down a long, dimly lit hallway into a room which was clearly the interrogation room. There was a single, eggshell colored table in the center of the room and two matching chairs. A large mirror, perched on the wall, obviously served as a one way window.

"Have a seat." Luke did as he was instructed.

"Ok, Mr Meier, I am going to need you to talk me through your day. From the moment you got up until you the moment you discovered Miss Hill's body."

Luke began to describe the day's events in vivid detail. Once he was done the detective asked, "Does your business have security cameras anywhere?"

"Yes, There is one located at the outside front entrance and one is also located on the outside of the side entrance. The side entrance is where I exited when I went to do the merchandise inventory that evening." Harper responded,

"Great, then we should be able to verify fairly quickly that you were indeed outside during the time of Miss Hill's murder."The interview continued for about another forty minutes and then he was excused. The moment he could, he went back to Cosette's side. Cosette was immediately called in. Luke protectively stood next to her and pleaded to go in and support Cosette during her interview. The detective chuckled,

"How chivalrous of you but that isn't how things work around here." With that, Cosette followed the detective to the same interrogation room as Luke had just been interviewed in.

"Ok, Mrs DuPont, let's get right down to business."

Cosette had to walk through every detail of her day as well. She omitted the part of when she got to the time of the evening when she was driving to the Watering Trough and received the text from Maggie. Her mind struggled heavily as to whether not mentioning the text was the correct to thing to do. She finally decided that she was not about to throw the man she loved to the wolves. She knew from the bottom of her soul that Luke was a kind, good hearted man. In fact, he was greater than any person she had ever known. She refused to believe that he would even want to harm a fly. She felt somewhat guilty for not mentioning Maggie's concerning texts, but she convinced herself that it would be wrong to mention it. Approximately an hour later, she was excused from the interview and went back to the waiting room. Luke was waiting anxiously for her. With concerned eyes, he asked her how the interview had gone.

"As good as expected. I can't believe my best friend is gone." She collapsed in a state of exhaustion into his arms and he held her tightly.

Luke insisted that she stay at his home that night. He sensed her hesitation.

"Listen, Cosette. There is a maniac running around out there. You are dreaming if you think I am not going to keep a close eye on you, at least until he or she is caught. I have a few guest rooms you can choose from. I think you will find them quite comfortable." Cosette couldn't resist his offer. She felt paralyzed with grief and scared senseless because a murderer was on the loose. Her emotions were a very painful mix. They drove back to his home. Luke assured her that he had a top notch security system in place at his residence.

"I am not really good about turning the system on but I sure will from now on." Cosette agreed that it was essential to set the alarms from this point forward. He showed her the room he found to be the most comfortable. It consisted of a queen-size, sleigh bed, crisp linens and overstuffed pillows adorned with pale green, silk pillow cases. The lighting was soft and soothing. The views out of the large windows were striking viewpoints of the expansive desert. She thanked him plenteously. He then proceeded on to his own bedroom. Cosette fell onto the bed in a sobbing heap.

"How could this have happened? How could Maggie be dead?" The permanency of the situation began to sink in and overwhelm her. She spent the night in and out of a fitful sleep. She endured one nightmare after the next but none of the dreams were quite as awful as the reality. Cosette woke up already reduced to tears. Panic and pain hijacked her heart.

In the morning, she called Chad and explained what had happened to Maggie. For once, he actually showed a hint of empathy and his voice was warm and reassuring. She explained to him that as desperate as she was to have Spencer with her full time, she could never put him in harm's way. They both agreed that until the murderer was caught, Spencer needed to stay with his father in Seattle. Cosette was scheduled to work a flight in two days. She called the airline and reported to them that Maggie had been murdered. After expressing their shock and condolences, they confirmed that she could schedule as much time off as she needed.

Luke came to check in on her mid morning. He even brought her a large glass of freshly squeezed orange juice and Egg's Benedict with fresh berries and whipped cream. She could not thank him enough for his kindness and hospitality. They talked for a while, each trying desperately to console the other. Then Luke's phone rang. Its clang pierced the air and disturbed their peaceful discussion. Luke grabbed the cell on the second ring.

"Luke here, how may I help you?" Cosette heard him say, "Ok," a handful of times. He ended the conversation with, "I'll be right down."

Cosette looked at him curiously and she asked what was going on.

"That was Detective Harper. She requested for me to meet her down at the station. Please come with me," he pleaded. "I really don't feel comfortable leaving you alone." Cosette agreed. They quickly got ready and drove to the station.

Upon arrival, Luke was quickly ushered into the interrogation room. Cosette sat nervously waiting in the reception area. She stared blankly at the heavily worn formica floor. Her normally twinkling, expressive eyes were dark pools of fear and fatigue. Luke sat down at the table and Harper commenced the interview.

18

"Mr. Meier, we have a problem. Investigators tried to view the security footage from your cameras. Both had been disabled. I find that very odd. Don't you?"

"What? That's impossible."

"Oh, it's possible, sir. Actually, it is more than possible. It's a fact. I am going to have to ask you to stay in the area. Something tells me this will be one of many interviews."

"I hope you are not implying that I am a person of interest?"

"Every one becomes a person of interest in a situation like this. Here's the bottom line. You were the last person to see Miss Hill and you were the first one to discover her body. We are early on in the investigation but I need to reiterate again that you are not to the leave the town limits." Luke agreed and, of course, emphasized that he was as determined as anyone to find the pig who did this. He insisted that he would do anything to cooperate and make the investigation easier.

The interview concluded and he exited the building with Cosette. He told her every detail of what was said during the interview. Cosette was overcome with fear. She tried to self soothe by wrapping her arms around herself. Nothing could happen to Luke. She had no doubt he was innocent but she also knew how innocent people have tragically gone to prison at times. That just couldn't happen to him. They went back to his home and sat together in somber silence.

Lucy had been poring over wedding magazines all morning. She was so excited to marry the love of her life, Austin. She added her favorite photos to her Pinterest account. Photos of luscious veils, alluring dresses and exotic honeymoon locales littered her account. Their wedding was only two months away. She couldn't believe that the day was almost here. She would finally become Mrs. Lucy Jolin. Just the thought of it sent goosebumps up and down her spine. She had an appointment for a dress fitting later that afternoon. Her dreamy thoughts were interrupted by a harsh knock on her townhome door.

"Could it be Austin?" She opened the door and a lady she had never seen before was standing there with a firm hand on her hip.

"Hello, are you Lucy London?"

"I am," replied Lucy timidly. The lady flashed her badge at Lucy. Sun rays glinted off of its metal.

"I am Detective Harper Metcalf. May I come in?" Lucy was startled but, of course, obliged.

"Yes, please come in. Have a seat." She pointed to the love seat adorned with a tiny rose print pattern. She felt embarrassed by the bridal magazines strewn messily on top of the coffee table. Once both ladies sat down, Harper immediately began her line of questioning.

"I would like to know what you did throughout the day yesterday." She glanced down at her notebook. "I would particularly like to know the details of your whereabouts between the hours of 6pm and one this morning." Lucy couldn't mask her confusion and concern.

"May I ask what this questioning is in regards too?" she inquired politely.I would like you to answer my questions first, please."

"Ok," Lucy thought back to the events of the day before. "I had the day off. I visited my parents in South Lake Tahoe. I went there in the morning at about 10:00 a.m. and returned at about 7:00 p.m. My sister just had a baby. So, we were spending the day together as a family, enjoying my new, little niece."

"Congratulations! Sounds like a nice day. What did you do after you left your parents and sister?"

"I made the drive back to my townhome. I stopped about thirty minutes before I got home and picked up dinner at the Sonic Drive thru. I drove directly home after that. I ate my dinner and then I binge watched "Yes, to the Dress. I'm getting married in two months!" Lucy exclaimed excitedly. The detective asked her,

"That's wonderful. Who is the lucky man?"

"Austin Jolin." Lucy's eyes glowed. Harper could see how much she adored him. Harper continued.

"Did you, at any point, see your fiancee yesterday?

"No, I didn't. This questioning is starting to scare me. What is going on?" Harper ignored Lucy's inquiry,

"Did he ever communicate with you in any way?

"Of course, we usually text each other throughout the day. He even called me at around 9:00 p.m."

"How was his tone during the conversation and how long did the call last?"

"He sounded tired but happy and very loving. We talked for about ten minutes." Harper knew she had to break the news to this seemingly sweet, unsuspecting girl.

"Are you aware that there was a murder here in town late last night?" Lucy gasped and the color drained from her face.

"How is this possible? It's a small town. Word travels at lightning speed usually. Who was killed?"

"A young lady by the name of Maggie Hill. She was murdered at the "Watering Trough late last night." Lucy felt weak in the knees.

"I had no idea! How tragic. She was such a sweet girl. She had her entire life in front of her still!" Harper asked pointedly,

"Have you spoken to Austin today yet?" Lucy's face flushed with embarrassment,

"Not yet. He tends to sleep in." Harper stood up and said that was all the questions she had for now. She handed Lucy her card. "If you think of anything, anything at all, please contact me immediately."

"Of course," Lucy stuttered. She was visibly shaken and her slim legs wobbled. At that, the detective left her home and Lucy remained seated and felt her perfectly manicured hands trembling.

19

Harper walked to her car, deep in thought,
"That liar, Austin, told us he was with his
fiancee last night. That obviously isn't true. I will
need to interview him again." She then darted
back to the station to have a meeting with Jasper
and Kelly. They had a lot to talk about.

Harper entered the conference room like a
woman on a mission. Jasper and Kelly were
already seated at the table and reviewing their
notes. They both had lattes in front of them. They
even had a third one waiting for Harper. Jasper
handed it to Harper and said,

"You will need this. We are going to have a
very long night."Jasper walked over to the

whiteboard and began writing different names down.

Luke Meier
Cosette DuPont
Austin Jolin

"Okay, ladies, our list of people of interest is pretty short right now. We are going to comb this town over like a flea bitten dog and continue to add anyone who even blinks the wrong way onto the list. The last homicide our department dealt with was a murder/suicide. That was a pretty slam dunk case. Maggie Hill's murder feels like a whole different level to me." The detectives nodded in agreement. "We are dealing with all kinds of crazy when we have a killer who sticks a high heel from a shoe down a lovely, young woman's throat. It is premature to say this, but I am suspicious that her murder could be the work of a serial killer. The placing of the heel into her throat is what law enforcement would generally consider a signature move, which is very serial killer like. Kelly, I need you to contact Reno PD after our meeting. Tell them we need any manpower they can part with to help patrol our streets. Our town is known as a cute, old west, silver mining town. We don't need it to become the serial killer capital of the USA. Now let's talk about Luke Meier first. It's very suspicious to me that both of his security cameras were disabled at the time of the murder. Plus, he was the last person to see Miss Hill alive and he just happened to again be the individual who actually discovered her dead body. That's not a good look for him."

Harper interrupted, "Jasper, I agree with everything you are saying but I just came from an interview with Lucy London, Austin Jolin's fiancee. Basically, the alibi he gave us is a bunch of bullshit. He was nowhere near his fiancee last night. This caught the attention of Jasper and Kelly.

"Oh wow," Kelly exclaimed,

"We need to keep a close eye on him. Let's get him back here for another interview. Offer him a drink. I want his DNA. If he refuses a drink, watch to see if he is chewing gum or takes a smoke during his breaks."

"Consider it done," the detectives responded in unison.

20

A few days passed. A hushed silence covered the town. People made sure to set their home alarms and to lock their doors. Children were not allowed to walk to friends' homes or go to the park unattended. Fear was the prevailing emotion among the citizens. Lucy kept texting and calling Austin. He barely answered her. She felt crushed. She loved him so deeply but she felt like he was starting to pull away from her.This destroyed her. He finally agreed to come over on Saturday evening. Lucy wanted to ask him why the detective had questioned her so much. She prepared his favorite meal, Fettuccini Alfredo, garlic bread and a salad, straight from her garden. She lit candles and sprayed the home, as always, with a vibrant, clean smelling, orange citrus scent. When he finally arrived, she fell into his arms. and sighed. She couldn't help it. Everything about him made her crazy with love and desire. She planted a passionate kiss on his beautiful lips and she was relieved to see that he was responding and kissing her back. She had missed him so much. It was unlike them to go days without seeing each other. First, they talked about the detective's visit. Austin explained that he was only being questioned because he visited Luke at that time. Since he was in the area at the time of the murder, it was standard to interview him as well. He emphasized that even Cosette was getting questioned because she was at the restaurant around the time of the murder. This put Lucy's mind at ease somewhat. His explanation made a lot of sense to her.

They enjoyed their lunch and then kissed and cuddled like teenagers for hours. Lucy was floating by the time Austin left. He promised he would visit her again the following day.

"I'm going to hold you to that, baby. I love you so much, Austin."

"I love you too, Lucy" He leaned in for one more passionate kiss and then he left. Lucy cleared the table and starting filling the dishwasher when she heard a light knock. She was so excited. Austin must have come back. She swung open the door and knew immediately that this was not a friendly visit. A cloaked but familiar face pushed his way in and held the meat tenderizer high above his head. Lucy screamed,

"You would never hurt me. I know you wouldn't. You're better than this. I know that you are a good person." He laughed and said,

"You are an even bigger idiot than I realized." He pummeled her with his weapon and the bride to be fell onto the floor. She was dead in an instant. He was thrilled to have an extra heel in his pack. He knew that Lucy was the type to wear flats, especially in her own home. He loved the crisp snap of the heel as he broke it off. He forced Lucy's mouth open and shoved the shiny heel deep into her throat.

"Good riddance! Too bad you didn't survive to the wedding day." His laugh was uproarious. "I really should have gone into comedy," he thought. "Letterman has nothing on me." He retreated into the chilling night, whistling in the most spine chilling way. He felt rejuvenated by the murder he had just committed.

21

Cosette and Luke had been joined at the hip since Maggie's tragic murder. They spent their days in deep conversation, cooked meals together and lounged by the pool. Their love grew deeper with each passing day. However, they both held back from taking their friendship to the next level. As desperate as they were to become lovers and more, they both knew it was just plain wrong. After all, Cosette was still legally married and had a young son to think about. Added to the disastrous mix, was the horrendous death of Cosette's best friend. Although hearing a description of the days they shared together gave the impression of joy and good times, the truth is they were both under horrible duress. They were not only grieving Maggie's death but they were in a constant state of high anxiety because of the regular detective interviews they were summoned to attend. Despite their deep love for one another, this was far from the ideal time to embark on a romantic relationship together. Many a nights, it took every ounce of willpower for Cosette not to visit Luke's room. She knew it was the wrong thing to do. She would use any tactic imaginable to refrain from making this drastic error. And Luke's temptation was even more amped up than Cosette's. He had never been consumed by such extreme love and desire. He ached for her. He needed her. He worshipped her and he had to spend the rest of his life with her. A lifetime would still not be enough time for his liking. However, he was a moral and good man. He respected her with every ounce of his being. She was deeply grieving right now. Cosette needed a true friend, at this point, not a lover. That would only confuse the situation. He would much rather be patient now and wait for the right time. He needed her for a lifetime not just for a night of passion. Wyatt, Luke's cousin, had been a huge support for both of them since Maggie's demise. In fact, Cosette was in the kitchen now preparing a pitcher of margaritas for his arrival. Luke was prepping the filet mignons at the poolside kitchen. With his wealth, he could grill them anyway he wanted to but he preferred them old school. He could have used his Kalamazoo grill but instead he grilled them over glowing briquets in his Weber kettle. This method always gave him the desired results. His mouth watered as the high end meats' aroma wafted up at him. He could hear the doorbell ring. Moments later, Cosette and Wyatt walked down the spiral staircase towards him. His cousin had a way of brightening his day. Wyatt had always been fiercely loyal to him. He had a great sense of humor and he was an attentive listener. The best part was that Wyatt had been exceptionally tender and supportive to both Cosette and to him since Maggie's murder. Family was everything to Luke and he was praying the day would come where he could add his beloved Cosette to their happy mix.

The meat was mouth watering. Plenty of garlic, onions and red pepper flakes were added. He prepped the baked potatoes with rich butter, chives and sour cream. The asparagus was crisp, flavorful and salted impeccably. Cosette delivered the pitcher of margaritas and two Pinot Noir bottles to the rectangular, grey, pedestal style table. Cosette and Luke had been favoring Pinot Noir over other types of wines because it had the highest concentration of the highly touted antioxidant resveratrol. This ingredient worked very well to lower both blood pressure and cholesterol. The wine's delicious taste served as an extra benefit. They relished the meal. It was cooked flawlessly. They purposely steered the conversation away from poor Maggie. Their talk was light and fun natured. After, they retreated to the seating area. Wyatt settled into a very comfortable teak lounge chair. Cosette and Luke sat on the all weather wicker, cream colored day bed adjacent to him. They continued drinking and chatting. The sun was beginning to set. Orange and dark yellow streaks decorated the sky. It reminded Cosette of burning embers and ripe tangerines.The sky in front of them was set ablaze. The distant desert was swabbed in colors of expansive gold. The openness of the landscape before them was awe inspiring. The town below them began to illuminate. The street lanterns sparked to life. The night sky became aglow with lights from the windows of the Virginia City homes. They could hear the occasional howling of faraway coyotes. The full moon shone brighter than an airport's runway lights. They basked in the peaceful final hours of the day. They almost forgot that a killer was on the loose.

22

He wandered the streets of the town aimlessly. He felt an aching restlessness which almost pushed him over the brink of insanity. His inner demons were back in full force and working over time. His urge had quieted for a couple of years when he transitioned from his truck driving job to moving back into town. He had to kill those two women in the past week. It was all part of an elaborate plan. He just didn't expect it to whet his appetite for killing again. These uncontrollable urges were not convenient for his current lifestyle. It was one thing when he regularly drove over numerous state lines. However, it was not quite as convenient now that he was permanently stationed in his hometown. He couldn't get sloppy. He had a perfect record so far. In fact, if they handed out olympic medals to serial killers, he would earn the platinum award every single time. He made Ted Bundy and Jeffrey Dahmer look like a couple of bumbling fools in comparison. He knew he was exceptionally intelligent. He was a star at everything he set his mind to and every moron he came into contact with was riveted by his charm and strong social skills.

"They were all a bunch of idiots!" He also was aware that, unfortunately, with all the new forensic evidence techniques coming forward in the last few years, he had to be extra cautious. He hated those damn DNA tests relatives were giving each other lately for birthdays and Christmases. For the past few years, as he sat with his family around the Christmas tree, he was sweating profusely in fear that they may "surprise" him with one of those kits. So far, luck had been on his side. However, all it would take is some darn fifth cousin to take part in the test, and he could possibly get tied to one, or even several, of his murders through DNA. His life would be destroyed. His idol, "The Golden State Killer" had been brought down as a result of one of those despicable genetic tests. That gentleman's downfall had been such a shame. He was his hero. That killer's arrest humbled him and reminded him that he needed to use all of the precautions necessary.

23

Austin woke up in his messy, fleece sheeted, twin bed earlier than normal. It was 9:00 a.m, just about two hours before he would normally wake up. He was scheduled to visit Lucy at lunch time. He still had a few more hours. Austin couldn't believe that he would be Lucy's husband in just two more months. That idea would have scared him to death a few years ago. Now the thought filled him with happiness. She made him feel complete and loved. He worshipped the very ground she walked on. But he was feeling enormous guilt about a recent indiscretion. His immoral actions sickened him. He could lose

Lucy forever if she ever discovered the truth. He tried to calm himself down. "You just won't let it ever leak. You've got this. It's in the past. It was a one time, stupid as all hell thing to do, and it will never, ever happen again."

He knew he would be the most loyal and doting husband. Their wedding day could not get here soon enough. He was even more excited for the honeymoon. They splurged on a, once in a lifetime, trip. They were going to Bora Bora and vacation at the enchanting Four Seasons Resort. Their nights would be spent in one of those overwater bungalow suites. He read that the bathroom even had a window on the floor so they could spot a variety of fishes and coral reefs with a variety of colors from the oversized tub. They could swim and snorkel right out front, in their own little lagoon. His head was swimming with all the possibilities his upcoming nuptials would bring. They had recently agreed that they would try to start a family soon after they retuned from their trip. Lucy had been dreaming of becoming a mom since she was at least a pre teen. Now, Austin was eager to become a dad as well. He tried to picture what their kids would look like. He hoped they looked just like Lucy. She had the cutest and most delicate features. More importantly, he hoped they would get her kind heart. His fiancee was one of a kind. He knew he was the luckiest man on Earth. He dragged himself out of his toasty bed and jumped into the shower.

At noon sharp, Austin knocked on Lucy's door. There was not a response. He knocked again.

"Hello? Lucy? Are you in there?" He texted her, "Baby, I'm here. Where are you?" Again, there was nothing but silence. He riffled through his overstuffed pant pockets and pulled out his key chain. He had about as many keys as a janitor. "I know Lucy's keys are here somewhere." He finally located them. He knocked one more time and then he let himself in. He immediately felt uneasy. The air was stale which was so unlike Lucy. She was religious about keeping her windows open during the day so the townhome had fresh air and she loved using her citrus spray as an added touch. He called out her name. He did not hear a response. Austin suppressed a shiver. As he glanced around the poorly lit room, his heart suddenly lurched. His angel was face up and appeared lifeless.

"Lucy?" He ran to her and, to his horror, it was clear that she was deceased. Her skin was completely drained of color and she was icy to the touch. He was in an utter state of panic. Austin grabbed his phone and dialed 911. His voice was thick with dread. Then he collapsed into a destroyed heap next to her. All at once, his stomach clenched and he started to heave and cry in hysterical wails. Just as had been the case with Maggie Hill's murder, ambulances and patrol cars arrived at the residence at a furious pace. The townhome was swarmed within minutes. Austin was removed from next to Lucy's body and taken to the hospital for observation. He was numb and had difficulty walking. His legs wobbled and he was weighed down by an emotional pain he never knew was humanly possible. He was placed on a stretcher and taken to the nearest hospital. They transported him into the emergency room and started IVs. He was dehydrated from excessive vomiting. Austin was in a perpetual state of high level panic. Finally, nurse at the critical care facility injected him with a strong sedative. He was so severely amped up that the medication took longer to kick in than it normally would have with a patient of his approximate size and weight. After about an hour, he collapsed into a deep slumber. As he drifted off, he was thinking that he was no different from an animal in Africa's Serengeti Park who needed to get darted in order to get it to comply. They literally put him out of his misery…temporarily.

Austin slowly woke up. He rolled his neck from side to side. He felt like he had been asleep for days. In actuality, he had only been asleep for about five hours. He slowly opened his eyes. It was a struggle because his eyelids were resisting as if they were taped shut. He felt confused and the room was spinning and blurry. He saw a vague figure in front of him. After a few minutes of laying there stationary, reality began to sink in. Lucy was gone. A sharp, searing pain shot through his heart. His vision became increasingly clearer. A lady was about five feet to the right of him. He knew she looked familiar but he could not quite place where he had seen her before. Austin still felt very groggy. He heard her start to talk to him.

"Mr. Jolin? Are you able to hear me? This is Detective Metcalf." She waited patiently for his response.

"Yes, I can hear you." His heart started to pound forcefully in his chest. Tears welled up in his eyes and dripped aimlessly down his cheeks. His lips trembled and they were turned downward. His chin quivered. The reality of what had happened to Lucy was sinking in deeper with each passing moment. He longed to be sedated again. Austin started nervously hitting the nurse call button repeatedly. He could feel he was beginning to become unglued again. The nurse shot into his room and asked if everything was ok.

"I need more sedation and I need it now!"

"Unfortunately, Mr. Jolin, Detective Harper will need to interview you first. They need you to be lucid. Then I will be happy to administer another dose." Austin did not have the strength to argue with the nurse. She excused herself and left the room. Detective Metcalf approached his bed.

"First, I would like to offer my deepest condolences for your loss. Unfortunately, I do have to conduct an interview since Lucy's death is now part if an active murder investigation." Austin's clammy skin had goose bumps on top of goose bumps. He felt nauseous. He vowed to himself that he needed to keep it together and answer the lady's questions. Whomever hurt his love, needed to pay for it. If he had to spend the rest of his life looking for her killer, he would. The detective seated herself. She had a laptop cradled in her lap and an extra large mug of coffee on the side table next to her.

"We have a big problem, Mr Jolin. A very big problem!" He barely had the strength to mutter,

"What's that?" but somehow he was able to spill his short response out.

"After Maggie Hill's murder you claimed that you were with your fiancee, Lucy, during the hours of the murder in question. That was your alibi. Did you really think we wouldn't go and check out your story?" He didn't even feel fear that he was caught lying. He was way past that. His life was already over without Lucy in it. "We NEED to know where you were specifically during the time of Maggie's slaying. Our station is now dealing with not only one but two brutal murders of young ladies. The fact that you lied about where you were during Maggie Hill's murder puts you at the top of our person of interest list. It sure doesn't help that you were the last one to see your fiancee either. Mr. Jolin, what is going on? I need answers right now." The guilt attacked Austin's chest. It took all of his strength to refrain from throwing up again.

"There is a reason I didn't want to say where I was the night of Maggie's murder. I was so scared of losing Lucy in case the details got back to her. I would have rather faced jail time than to lose her. She was my life."

"I'm listening," snapped the detective.

"Ok, here goes, I can barely admit it out loud. One of my closest friends, Shane, lives in Reno. We have been friends for years. After picking up a bottle of brandy at a downtown store in Virginia City that evening to bring to his house, I made the trek to Reno and visited him. We got pretty plastered. He started teasing me, asking me how it felt to know that I'd have my own ball and chain in a couple of months and that I would never be permitted to go near another woman again. So, I did something which I will regret for the rest of my life. We went to a brothel in Sparks. I guess the rest is kind of self explanatory." Tears flooded his face. His gut wrenched. Metcalf replied,

"I am going to need to know the name of the worker who you spent time with and I need to know the exact hour you arrived at this establishment and at what time you left, any stops you made on the way home. I need every detail." He gave her all the information he could recall. Metcalf ended their interview. She went out to her Honda Civic and drove directly to the brothel Austin had named in Sparks. She was not about to assume his story was true.

Detective Metcalf drove the distance to Sparks and pulled into the large parking area of the establishment. She knew this brothel all too well. It was notorious for being run by an old, ruthless lady, Madam Tina. The building consisted of three stories. The outside paint job reminded her of a birthday cake. It was entirely pink and white. Every window was darkened with thick drapes to ensure privacy.

"Here goes," Harper thought to herself. She walked up the well lit stairs and entered the heavy, wooden front doors. The interior was dimly lit with pink lightbulbs. Candles littered the large entry room. The stench of cigarette smoke was intense. Harper could feel her lungs being polluted just moments after entering the room. A number of ladies were waiting in the entry area. Each one was scantily clad. They were polite to her. Harper asked if Madame Tina was in tonight. One of the girls responded,

"This is your lucky day. She goes around to four different businesses so you are really fortunate that she is here right now. I can show you to her office."

"That would be helpful. Thank you." They walked down a long, heavily used carpeted hallway. The lady helping her knocked on the door at the end of the hallway. Harper heard a harsh, scratchy voice crow,

"Come in." The lady left Harper, at that point, and Harper entered the large, impressive office. Madam Tina was dressed in a glossy, silk, purple jumpsuit. Her nails were perfectly manicured. She had several large, multi colored rings on her fingers. Her hair was ruby red and her hair length was at chin level. She appeared confused by Harper's visit but she remained courteous. "How may I help you?" They exchanged introductions. Harper explained her dilemma and asked to see surveillance footage from the night of Maggie's murder. That's when Tina started to clam up.

"I would love to help you. I really would but one of the highlights of my thriving business is our discretion. We put our customers' privacy at the highest priority. So unless, you come back here with a search warrant, I will be unable to comment about Austin Jolin or any other client. The same goes for our security footage." Harper had feared this would happen.

"I understand. I will be back tomorrow with the required paperwork."

"That is fine. Let me check my schedule." Tina looked down at her planner. "I will be at this location tomorrow from 5:00 p.m. to 11:00 p.m." They bid one another a good evening and Harper drove back to the station.

24

Cosette knew it sounded silly but she truly missed seeing her roadrunner, Romeo. She was thrilled when Luke suggested that they should regularly visit the cottage in order to water the plants and do basic maintenance. Since she normally saw him in the morning hours, she suggested that they go to the cottage at around 7:00 a.m. Luke seemed a little confused.

"Isn't that kind of early?" he inquired suspiciously. Cosette laughed and knew it was time to fess up. After all, she worshipped this man and he was her best friend.

"Ok, I'll spill it. When Maggie and I were living at the cottage, I had a daily visitor and I kind of fell in love with him." Luke looked insanely jealous and concerned.

"Oh?" ,he said sounding brokenhearted.

"Every morning, this darling roadrunner would visit me. He would sunbathe, drink and I even fed him". She admitted the last part guiltily because she knew it was not wise to feed wild animals.Luke laughed and felt a huge sense of relief that she was not referring to a gentleman caller.

"A bird?" ,Luke exclaimed. Cosette replied,

"Hey, he isn't just any bird. He is my bird. I even named him Romeo." Luke laughed heartily for the first time in weeks. Then Cosette joined in. This was the happiest and most carefree they had felt since Maggie's tragic demise.

"Well, if my Cosette wants to see her darling Romeo, then we will most certainly go at the time when he calls." They both erupted into laughter.

They left Luke's home at dawn. Cosette couldn't believe that she was about to be reunited with her precious Romeo. They entered the cottage and Cosette dashed to her former bedroom. She peered out her window. He was nowhere in sight. She waited. In the meantime,

Luke watered the plants. Suddenly, she saw her little rascal emerge from the shrubs. Her heart skipped a beat. She knew that the flat terrain and dry brush of the backyard had initially attracted him. She went to a bird shop in Reno after a flight one day and stocked up on various types of bird seed. She also fed him a variety of fruits. That seemed to hook him in. Every single day they would meet up. He relished the food she gave him. Occasionally he would scoop up a lizard in the backyard. She tried not to watch the brutality of it but she still loved him. The roadrunner seemed very calm and relaxed around her while he was sunbathing. Luke sat next to her and watched Romeo's antics. Cosette could tell he was getting pulled in by the roadrunner's charms also.

25

All the investigators met for an extra intense, meeting at the station. Jasper, Kelly, Harper and three additional FBI agents were huddled around the conference table. It was horrible enough to have a single murder in a small town. However, now they were dealing with two women within less than a week who had been bludgeoned to death. Both had heels inserted into their throats. This investigation had officially been upgraded from a murder investigation to a "serial killer being on the loose" investigation. The similarities between both murders could not be ignored. They contained the same signatures, same type of weapon and it was even clear that the murderer was left handed in both cases.They were undeniably dealing with one specific individual. If he had already struck twice, he would inevitably strike again. They even called in a top forensic psychologist from the East Coast. Dr. Marie Johnson was at the very top of her field. She did her undergraduate work at the University of Oregon. After that she specialized in Forensic Psychology and received her doctoral degree from Drexel University in Philadelphia.This was her expertise, her lifelong passion, study and research. She had zero doubt, once she was presented with all of the facts, that the murderer was indeed a serial killer. More than likely, he had killed many times prior to Maggie Hill's murder. The psychologist was even more certain that the killings would continue. Dr. Johnson emphasized to the group that a killer was not officially classified as a "serial" killer until he or she committed three or more murders. Up to this point, they could only confirm that this individual had murdered two people. Nonetheless, she was willing to bet her degrees that he had definitely already killed far more people than Maggie Hill and Lucy London.

Dr. Johnson walked up to the white board and wrote down the four different types of serial killers.

Visionary
Mission-oriented
Hedonistic
Power/Control

Based on the evidence she was presented with so far, she was quite certain that these murders were power and control based. Just the act of inserting a heel into a deceased person's throat demonstrated complete power. The corpse has zero control over what is happening to him or her. Dr Johnson continued with her analysis. More than likely the killer is a caucasian male who is exceptionally intelligent in his own twisted way. He probably is "hiding in plain sight". What this means is that he is perceived as a normal, or even a charismatic citizen. Nobody would ever suspect him. He has seemingly standard social interactions and relationships. Dr Johnson noted that it was glaringly obvious that since absolutely no DNA was retrieved from the bodies, that he is a highly organized and experienced killer. There were no fingerprints on the scene, no hair, saliva or DNA from other bodily fluids.This is an individual who knows what he is doing. These murders were not spur of the moment events. He calculated them down to every last detail. He received a great deal of satisfaction and feelings of grandeur from the murders. Based on the way the victims were bludgeoned, the angle, intensity of the hit, she would estimate the killer to be taller than six feet. Probably even between 6'2 and 6'4. Research indicates that upwards of 70% of serial killers have repeated substance abuse issues, so don't let that slip from your radar. He probably encountered childhood abuse and trauma himself. Experiences during infancy and childhood hold the key in forming future serial killers. Their mothers often encourage them to hate other females. These mothers tend to be excessively controlling, overprotective and even abusive. Future serial killers enjoy harming animals during their youth. Generally, after torturing animals, they then graduate to hurting humans. She advised them to search for any individuals who have a history of committing arson.

"They also had the tendency to be bed wetters as children but that would be harder to verify." This lightened the mood in the room momentarily and everyone at the table chuckled. "Jokes aside, these are all clues which will get us closer to ultimately

discovering who did these heinous slayings. We need to put the puzzle pieces together before he acts again. More than likely, the killer is not a tourist or a transient but rather a long term, established resident."

26

Harper retuned to the brothel with the search warrant in hand. The staff members were very cooperative. She was able to confirm that Austin Jolin was indeed at the establishment during the time frame of Maggie's murder. The surveillance cameras clearly showed him entering the brothel prior to the murder and then exiting a few hours later. The worker, who had spent time with him, was able to confirm that she was with him the entire time he was at the business. His alibi was airtight. He was no longer a person of interest for Maggie's death. Since Lucy's death had the same signatures such as the heel inserted into her throat, it was almost certain the same monster killed both ladies. Therefore, Harper was willing to bet that Austin had no involvement with either murder.

Law enforcement combed through Maggie and Lucy's cell phones. They inspected text messages, social media messages and their calendars. Anything which was inputted into those mobile devices was uncovered and analyzed. One communication came back glaringly suspicious and could prove to be potential evidence. A text message had been sent around Maggie's time of death from her cell. She had sent the text to her best friend, Cosette DuPont. The text message claimed that Luke Meier's behavior was concerning. Maggie seemed to be uncomfortable around him.Harper traced back through the notes from Cosette's interview. She was 99% sure that Cosette had failed to mention this key text. Harper wanted to be absolutely sure that this was the case. After closely inspecting her notes, Harper was able to confirm that Cosette, did indeed, never mention the ominous text. She called Cosette and requested that she come down to the police station immediately. Cosette was cooperative and agreed but the inflection and tone of her voice showed signs that she was clearly nervous and hesitant.

Approximately, a half hour later, the receptionist notified Harper that Cosette was in the waiting area.

"Please escort her back to the interrogation room." A minute later, Cosette entered the room. Harper thought enviously, "She really is a strikingly beautiful woman. She's one of those rare women who wakes up in the morning looking like she's ready for a magazine cover shoot."

"Mrs. DuPont, please have a seat." Cosette obediently obliged.

"First, I want to thank you for getting to the station so quickly with such short notice. It is appreciated. I just wanted to go over the evening of Maggie Hill's death with you again. Please walk me through your entire day. It is critical that you not omit a single detail regardless of how trivial you may think it is."

Cosette began to recount her day. She appeared anxious as she spoke. To Harper's disappointment, once she had completed recalling her activities and occurrences of the day, she once again had left out the alarming text she received from the murder victim. Harper's voice became more stern and more direct.

"Did you receive any text messages from Maggie?" Cosette looked down. Her hands started mildly trembling. She did not answer. The room was so quiet that one could hear water running at the opposite end of the station.The detective stalled and eventually said,

"I need an answer from you." Cosette responded hesitantly.

"Yes, I did."

"And you didn't feel it was important to report this to us? I asked you now, not once but twice. What did the texts from her say?" Defeatedly, Cosette described the alarming texts. Harper continued,

"Why did you not mention this before? Clearly these texts of alarm from a soon to be murder victim are critical pieces to the puzzle."

"I did not mention it because I know for a fact that Luke Meier is an extremely kind hearted and gentle man. He even removes spiders he finds in his home by gently placing them outside on a shaded plant. I felt as if I would have thrown him under the bus if I were to mention these texts."

"What is the nature of your relationship with Mr. Meier?"

"We are very good friends. He has even been protecting me since the two horrific murders in town."

"You are strictly friends? Do you have an intimate relationship with him as well?" Cosette answered confidently,

"We do not." Harper was skeptical. Mrs DuPont was sure going out on a limb for a man who was supposedly just a friend. She was going to keep an extra close eye on both Mr. Meier and Mrs. DuPont, The meeting adjourned. Harper thanked her for coming in. Cosette exited the building. The detective instantly called a couple of her buddies, Peter and Dale, in law enforcement. She explained the murder cases to them and then she requested that they tail both Cosette and Luke. They agreed. If they did as little as sneeze, the officers would see it. Dale agreed to tail Cosette. Peter was assigned to watch Luke.

27

As the evening turned into nighttime, Harper realized that she had not stopped working since 5:00 a.m. "Where did the hours go?" Her entire body felt achy from pure exhaustion. The computer screen became increasingly blurry. She knew it was time to call it a night and go home. She was not being productive at all at this point. Her bed sounded like the definition of heaven to her. It was calling her. She left the station and walked to her car. There was a vast blanket of stars above her. The night was crisp. There was a slight breeze which made her skin break out into cold shivers. An owl hooted in the distance. Her thirty minute drive back to her home in Reno felt like two hours. Her eyes felt dangerously heavy and fatigued. She opened all of her windows and blasted the radio. Her favorite DJs were on the air. They were a man/woman duo. Harper especially loved their nightly prank call segment. Tonight's episode was particularly funny. This kept her alert enough to safely make her way to her cozy and inviting home.

She drove into her garage. Her automatic front porch lights sprung to life. Harper entered her home and let out a sigh of relief. It felt wonderful to be in her two bedroom, two bath bungalow. She placed her large work backpack onto the entry area hanger. Harper was the ultimate master of organization. Everything had a place. She was unable to fall asleep at night until her belongings were all stored in their assigned spots. She went to the fridge and pulled out her favorite wine, a Cabernet from the Napa Valley. She poured herself a glass.

He waited.

"She's some detective. I had been watching for her in the parking lot. I then followed her since the moment she left the station. She is completely clueless. A four year old would be more alert to her surroundings than she is. Moron!"

Once he arrived at her house, he stayed in the background to remain undetected. The man parked parallel to the sidewalk, two houses up from hers. He slipped out of his car, eased the door shut. and walked silently up to her bungalow. Harper was visible through the front window. She was located in the kitchen. The room's lights were on full bright. The harsh glare reminded him of an airport runway. Crouching down in front of some shrubs which were dotting the perimeter of her front porch, he was on full alert and conscious of every sound. Detecting the far off pulsing wail of a police siren, he held his breath. The man felt somewhat safe knowing he was slumped in the shroud of shadows. He relished the secure feeling it gave him. A part of him always feared that a family member, friend or even an acquaintance would be able to detect that he was a killer. It coursed through his blood and down into his bones. Being a killer was his entire essence. He often laughed when he saw ads for Disneyland.

"Happiest place on earth? Ha! They had never experienced the ecstasy of a kill. It was unbeatable and the most intense high imaginable. Cocaine had nothing on it!" At this point, the night was completely still. He continued to watch.

The drink instantly calmed her frayed nerves. Harper sat at her small dining table and enjoyed the scarlet, velvety liquid as it soothed her parched throat. Suddenly she saw a movement at the kitchen window. She grabbed her gun, which was usually close by. She flipped off her lights so she would be able to see outside more clearly. Harper hugged the wall of the room and crept up to the side of the kitchen window. She peered out cautiously. The movement was distinct. She squinted and zeroed in on the figure. What she saw made her laugh. It was a beautiful, very well fed, orange cat. He stared at her with unblinking eyes. Harper had seen this oversized beauty before and always enjoyed watching his antics. He was an exquisite cat.

163

She longed to have a kitten of her own but knew that it would not be fair to a potential pet since her work kept her away from home a great deal of the time. She instantly relaxed, flipped on her lights and went back to her drink. Her fatigue was overwhelming. She took a long, hot shower. Her muscles relaxed. It almost felt like a spa day for her.

"Had it been that long since I have pampered myself, that I consider a regular shower to be a luxurious treatment?" Harper slipped into her lavender colored, silk pajama set and crawled into bed. It felt so wonderful. Her body had been aching all day long. Her eyes burned from relentless fatigue. Finally, she was content, warm and completely comfortable. She instantaneously drifted into a deep slumber.

Once the bungalow was enveloped in complete darkness, he knew it was time to make his move. There was only a sliver of a moon visible now. The clouds had moved in. He felt electrified and more alive once it was dark. He enjoyed how it shrouded him and made him undetectable.

"What a perfect night it is to take this sad and ridiculous detective's life". He slipped into her backyard. The decor was bland. There was a small, cheaply built patio table and two rickety appearing, white chairs around it. A small palm tree stood in one corner of the lot. A darkened lantern was the only decor he could see. He had become an expert at picking locks. The door entering into the bungalow was one of the easiest locks he had ever had to pick. He couldn't help but to smile when it cracked soundlessly open. He had done his share of research on the layout of the detective's home. He was far too experienced, at this point, to not research his intended victims down to the smallest details.

Before he went into Harper's bedroom, he gave himself a self guided tour of her home. With a gloved hand, he touched and smelled the various knick knacks throughout the family room, kitchen and spare bedroom. Undoubtedly, these items were precious to her. He detected a eucalyptus scent permeating from her belongings and throughout the home. It was all so fresh, almost woodsy. He felt intoxicated by the texture and fragrance in her home.

"Enough clowning around for now. You are here for a much greater purpose," he reminded himself. Her bedroom door was ajar. A sea shell shaped night light glowed faintly in the hallway. Her bedroom window contained thick, black out curtains.

"This girl likes it dark, just like me. "Who knows? Maybe I'm killing my own soulmate." He bit on his hand to avoid laughing out loud. He had always enjoyed his humor. He prided himself on being one of the funniest people to have ever inhabited the planet Earth. He really was an amazing man. Too bad that others weren't privy to some of his greatest talents. Once again, he fought back laughter.

He entered her room and heard soft snoring. The sound reminded him of a kitten purring. He walked over to her bed. She was sleeping on her stomach while holding a pillow under her chest.

"What a strange woman. She's a stomach sleeper. No wonder she has always been hopelessly single." He stared down at her sleeping figure for at least five minutes. He basked in each breath she took because he knew they were some of her very last. The power he held made him giddy and almost light headed. Finally, he spoke. He held the meat tenderizer tightly in his fist.

"Oh, sleeping beauty." No response. "Wow, I have a very tired girl to deal with." He said it again but this time louder. He expected her to slowly wake up but instead she bolted up. He had flipped on the hallway light before he entered her room. Her eyes quickly adjusted to the dark and she zeroed in on his face.

"You?" Recognition flooded across her face. Her skin transformed into a sickly, milk like color. A blood curling scream erupted from deep within her. Before she had time to reach for her gun on the night stand, he hit her violently on the center of her head. That distinctive cracking sound was one of his favorite parts...

Harper's survival instinct kicked into overdrive but it was pointless. It was too late. As she lay dying, her breathing became increasingly shallow. She could feel darkness starting to obscure her vision. Then she heard him whisper in an amused tone.

"Good riddance, princess. She took her final, rasping breath. The murderer took a moment to fully relish the crime he had just committed. After a few minutes, he knew it was time to go. The risk of getting caught would be too high if he continued to stay at Harper's residence. He exited her home under the cloak of darkness as he whistled quietly to himself.

28

Luke felt perpetually stressed out. The recent homicides had made him crumble emotionally. He also hated seeing Cosette so anxious and upset. He asked law enforcement if he was able to travel for a week to his vacation home in the Lake Tahoe area. After some hesitation, they gave him permission. He longed to distract Cosette and see her laugh again, the way she had been before Maggie's murder. He went to Cosette's room and told her the good news.

"We have both gone through a lot in the last month. I received permission from law enforcement for us to go to my vacation home in

Lake Tahoe and stay there for a while." Cosette's eyes lit up. Truth was, she was deeper in love with Luke than she ever knew imaginable. Her love strengthened on a daily basis. Yet, she was heartbroken about her best friend's murder. The grieving aspect was grueling enough on its own. It did not help that she and the love of her life were regularly being questioned by the authorities.

"Really, Luke? That would be a wonderful distraction. This trip's timing is especially perfect since I am still off of work."

"I agree, Cosette. Let's leave in the morning. It isn't a long drive." They both agreed and felt a happiness and excitement they had not felt since Maggie's demise.

The next morning, Cosette awoke, brushed her teeth, groomed herself and then headed out to the kitchen. She found Luke there, packing up food supplies and making sandwiches for their journey. She approached Luke and embraced him. This was more physical than they normally got. Cosette held him close. She was in heaven when she felt his strong, loving embrace.

"Luke, I need this getaway. I can't thank you enough for planning it and making it happen. It is so thoughtful of you." He brushed his soft lips against her neck and goosebumps erupted on her. She had truly never felt a love like this. Her love for him had the power to make her forget any worries or past pain she had ever experienced.

"Shall we hit the road?" Luke prompted Cosette. They jumped into Luke's convertible. On their way out of town, they stopped briefly to water the plants at his cottage and visit Romeo. He seemed excited to see them. Cosette fed him a hardy meal of nuts and seeds. When she was convinced that Romeo was satisfied, they commenced on their much needed road trip. The convertible top was put into the down position. It felt exhilarating for Cosette. They blasted her favorite tunes and admired the beautiful scenery as they passed by small, quaint towns and lakefront cafes. Her beautiful hair whipped around her bare shoulders. She couldn't help but think that this just felt so right. Her heart was full of love. She was jubilant, not a common feeling, especially recently, for Cosette to experience.

After some time, they arrived at Luke's lakefront home. It was located in the town of Rubicon, which was nestled along the western shore of Lake Tahoe. The beauty of Emerald Bay was hard to describe. Cosette had rarely seen such a picturesque landscape. Luke signaled right and pulled into a long, gated driveway. He punched in the code at the gate. It dutifully opened. He proceeded down the remainder of the private driveway and pulled up in front of the glorious home. Pine trees and a variety of other shrubs surrounded the home. Cosette could not help but sigh.

"What breathtaking beauty!" The home offered a lot of privacy. Cosette was unable to see the neighbor's homes. The entire area was heavily wooded. Cosette knew that this area was often described as the Black Forest of Lake Tahoe. She could certainly see that this was an accurate description. They departed the car with their luggage and walked towards the front of Luke's home. The inky blue water lapped at the shore directly in front of the home. A family of Canadian Geese were circling around the closest buoy. From a relatively short distance, Cosette spotted

Emerald Bay. Luke proudly told her that it was one of the most photographed locations on earth.

"Well, I can definitely see why," Cosette agreed.

They entered the home, both feeling giddy. It was a modern looking, 3,400 square foot house. Cosette loved that even though it was modern it still managed to be steeped in the charm of old Lake Tahoe. They were currently situated on the main level. It had an open floor plan, high vaulted ceilings and it boasted panoramic views of the majestic lake from its sparkling, gigantic windows. The turquoise water took Cosette's breath away. A large deck with a hot tub connected to the family room and kitchen area.

"We even get to enjoy 100 feet of lake frontage. We can go boating and water skiing tomorrow, if you'd like."

"Oh, I'd love that," gushed Cosette. For the first time since her best friend's murder, she felt relaxed and happy. Only Luke had the power to pull off such a miracle.

They got settled in their separate bedrooms, put on their swimsuits and then met downstairs on the expansive redwood deck. Luke started grilling prime rib and corn on the cob while Cosette worked on preparing the mashed potatoes. The sky was ablaze with the fire of the setting sun and it looked dramatic in hues of brilliant oranges and violets as if brushed upon an artist's canvas. The colors stretched far and wide. Cosette's eyes were steady to the horizon. Luke moved closer to her. She could feel the warmth of his body against hers. They both stayed quiet to allow each other to get lost in this magical moment. Everything felt so right. Even the water of the lake took on some of the hues from the sky. The subtle waves were tinged with streaks of purple and tangerine orange. The wind began to pick up. The surrounding trees and plants were lit up with a golden glow. It was all so breathtaking. Luke looked at Cosette and asked pleadingly,

"Are you thinking what I'm thinking?" Cosette giggled and asked nervously,

"What are you thinking?"

"Let's swim!" Cosette's face lit up.

"Yes, Let's!"

Luke grabbed her hand and they darted into the slowly darkening water. The gentle breeze created ripples onto the surface of the lake. They entered its crystal water. A feeling of pure serenity passed through both of them. The water surrounding Cosette's body was so cool and refreshing, yet, it was also relaxing. Her feet crunched into the cold, wet sand. She concentrated on the feeling of the minuscule grains on the floor of the lake. It felt like a form of therapy. She got lost in the sensations. They were completely alone. The only sound, at this point, was the heavy echo of a distant owl. Luke pulled her close to him. His body heat was her only relief from Lake Tahoe's frigid water. They held each other close. There was no space between them. Cosette knew that she would never forget this moment of togetherness with the love of her life. Cosette looked up at Luke timidly through her thick, midnight black lashes. Luke closed his eyes and leaned forward so he could be even closer to her. His gentle yet strong arms pulled her towards him. He whispered words into her ear, words she couldn't decipher. The couple's breathing patterns matched perfectly. She felt as if they were one. Luke resisted kissing her. He was desperate to but he didn't want to destroy the relationship they were slowly building. She was worth the wait. The sky rapidly darkened. Away from the city lights, the Milky Way was bright and intoxicating. The sky was brimming with puffy clouds and dramatic, shining stars. In the velvet dark, the crescent moon contrasted and was a twinkling white. The striking night scene above helped to halt the carousel of their never ending worries. Cosette felt a single raindrop on her cheek. The aroma from the nearby tall grasses served as an intoxicating perfume. The light wind continued to caress them. Cosette felt a vulnerability like she had never felt before. She knew that he had the power to crush her heart, her dreams and her future. Yet, when she looked up into his eyes, she felt an indescribable warmth and kindness. She sensed that he loved her. Was it possible that he really did love her or was this all wishful thinking?

"I set the hot tub to 100 degrees. Should we take a dip?" ,tempted Luke. Cosette welcomed the idea. They ran with their hands entwined up to the expansive deck and gently lowered themselves into the bubbling, steaming hot water. This was both of their definition of pure bliss.

29

Harper was due to attend a meeting at the station that morning at 9:00 a.m. The Forensic psychologist, Dr. Johnson, Jasper and Kelly were sitting around the conference room table nursing their steaming cups of coffee. They made small talk for a while and waited patiently for Harper's arrival.

"It is so unlike Harper to be late for anything," a concerned Jasper stated while looking at the time on his cell. They tried calling but were unable to reach her.

"She may be in an area with no cell reception. Let's wait another fifteen minutes. Unfortunately,

I cannot stay longer because, at that point, I will need to leave to go to a meeting in Carson City," reasoned Dr. Johnson. Traffic is supposed to be choppy. I can't wait much longer than that." The trio waited the additional time and then begrudgingly adjourned their meeting. They agreed to meet at the same time the following morning. Dr Johnson rushed to her meeting. Jasper and Kelly spent the morning interviewing a number of citizens in town in hopes of hammering down more details of the multiple killings.

By noon, Jasper returned to the station. He was alarmed when he was told that Harper had not yet arrived for work. Jasper picked up his phone and dialed the Reno PD.

"Good afternoon, Don. This is Jasper from Virginia City."

"Hey, Jasper. Good to hear from you. I bet you have work up to your elbows with the recent homicides in your town?"

"Yeah. It has been rough. I'm lucky if I get three hours of snooze time at this point. I need a favor. Detective Harper Metcalf is the lead detective working with me on these cases. She was supposed to be here this morning for a meeting. She never showed. Would you mind sending someone from your department to check on her? Her place is at 3520 Ivy Road. It isn't like her to not respond to our calls and texts."

"Consider it done. I have a couple officers in that area right now. I'll radio them to swing on by and check on her. I'll call you back when they get back to me." Don jumped up from his chair and immediately inputted the request into the computer aided dispatch system. Almost instantly, the police officers, Margo and Steve, saw his request on their Mobile data computer located in the patrol car.

They arrived at Harper's residence within two minutes. Steve knocked briskly on the door and rang the doorbell. After waiting a short time, they knocked again. In the state of Nevada, it is legal for officers to enter a residence for wellness checks without a search warrant. The front door was bolted shut but they noticed a window was open on the right side of Harper's home. It was a large, chest level window. Therefore, it was easy for Margo and Steve to prop themselves up on the sill and enter her home. Once inside, they were greeted by a stylish collection of beautifully framed family photographs. The photos served as a kaleidoscope of Harper's memories. The bed was tidy and unused looking. If someone had slept in this bed last night, there were no indicators of it. The large sleigh bed looked sumptuous and elegant. The sheets were a gleaming, pristine white. The entire room was immaculate. The sunlight peeked through the window and illuminated the sweet toffee browns of the hardwood floor.

As they cautiously moved into the hallway, Margo and Steve became bathed in a golden light. The seashell night light and the overhead recessed lights radiated brightly. The residence was shrouded in complete silence other than the chorus of blue jays drifting in through the open window. Directly across from the bedroom which they had just exited, stood another room. The thick curtains made the bedroom appear gloomy and cast in shadows. The fabrics in the room were muted hues. The officers entered the room. The air was stale and humid. Their high powered flashlights made the silhouettes in the room more discernible. Steve's eyes focussed on the spacious bed. He instantly saw a figure collapsed on the center of it. To both of their horrors, they spotted Harper on the bed. She was clearly deceased. Her eyes were gaping and lifeless. As the officers looked at her, they could see the heel of a stiletto plunged into her throat. Steve and Margo stared at each other in disbelief.

30

Nevada's Department of Public Safety was notified of Detective Metcalf's homicide. Since the same signature was left at each murder, they were convinced that this was the act of a serial killer. The fact that a stiletto heel had been lodged in the throat of all three victims, was kept strictly confidential. Therefore, the chance of Harper's homicide being a copy cat murder was slim to none. The FBI was contacted. They were asked to provide assistance and provide lab, database and any other associated services.

They arrived at the Reno police department by the very next day. Nina Sokolov departed Quantico, Virginia early in the morning. She worked for the FBI's Critical Incident Response

Group. Nina held a fixation for serial killers ever since her younger sister, Chloe, was abducted and killed by one at the age of fourteen. The monster was finally caught about nine years later. By then, he had murdered at least twenty teens, all residing in the state of Michigan. The victims were between the ages of thirteen and eighteen. They were generally petite sized. Their heights ranged from 5'3 to 5'6. Every single last one of them had light brown, long, wavy hair and blue eyes. When Nina lost her sister, she was destroyed. She became a shell of her former self. She vowed that one day she would dedicate her life's work to catching these repeat offenders. She went to the University of Michigan and completed her undergraduate degree in Criminology. Nina was always at the top of her class. She then completed a graduate degree in Computer Forensics at Johns Hopkins.

She will never forget the day she received the phone call. She was accepted to go into the FBI training. She went to Quantico for twenty weeks of intensive training where she perfected her firearm techniques. Hogan's Alley was her favorite part of the grueling schedule. It simulated a small town. Nina enjoyed sharpening her investigative techniques and defensive tactics in the pseudo town. So far, she had been able to conduct interviews with thirty-four of the most notorious serial killers.

31

His eyes snapped open and he looked over at his digital clock. It was 3:19 in the morning. The velvet darkness seeped through his slightly opened curtains. Upon waking up just now, he replayed his recent murders. What delicious visions they all were. He felt giddy and at peace when he thought of the lives he had taken. Unfortunately, his tranquility only lasted briefly. It did not take long for the familiar hunger to surge within him once again. His last three kills had not been as satisfactory as some of his more treasured ones from the past. He hated when they died too soon. The recent victims barely had any fight in them. They were completely caught off guard. They weren't challenging enough for him. It consoled him to realize that their deaths served an additional purpose. Any pleasure he derived from the acts were just an added bonus.

Nina landed at the Reno-Tahoe International airport and went straight to the car rental agency. They gave her a chalk white Chevy Malibu. She punched in the police department's address into the GPS. It was on Second Avenue. She was familiar with the area from a previous assignment she had been involved with. She drove the short distance and parallel parked on the cross street. Nina noted that the station looked like any typical urban police station. She went through the front doors and was greeted by a receptionist at the information desk.

Nina introduced herself to the employee. She guessed her age to be in her early 40s. She was slender and had black wavy hair and steel grey eyes. Her name tag stated, "Tammy". Tammy greeted Nina with a broad smile. She was very kind and welcoming. Nina explained the purpose of her visit. Tammy's eyes registered recognition.

It was obvious to Nina that the rash of slayings had become the talk of the police department and, more than likely, the talk of the entire county. Tammy escorted Nina down two short hallways until they reached an expansive conference room. Tammy whispered,

"They just started." Nina was not surprised that she was slightly tardy. Her flight had been delayed due to a storm in the Midwest.

Nina entered the room discreetly and quietly. She did not want to disturb the meeting in progress. The room was full of unfamiliar faces. An official looking gentleman was speaking and writing on the white board. The audience was listening intently. They all were sporting serious expressions. There was only one chair still vacant. Nina made a bee line for it and got settled. She gently pulled out her lap top and began to take notes. Nina soon discovered that the chief of the Reno Police Department was the speaker. He made it crystal clear that he was convinced that the recent string of murders was the work of a serial killer. The speaker was suddenly interrupted by a call on his cell. He asked for the meeting to break for about fifteen minutes. He swiftly exited the conference room. A handsome man was sitting directly next to Nina. She estimated that he was a few years older than she was. As soon as the unscheduled break commenced, he looked over at Nina. He smiled warmly and introduced himself.

"Hello, I'm Jasper. I am the sheriff in Virginia City." Nina couldn't help but to feel mesmerized by his warm, deep, brown eyes.

"Hi, my name is Nina Sokolov. I am with the FBI. I just flew in from Quantico."

"Wow, you have come a long way. I appreciate that. We can use all the help we can get. The residents of my town feel traumatized. We need to get this bastard." Nina heartily agreed. Just then the meeting started again.

The chief briefed the room on every detail of the recent murders. They all agreed that they were dealing with a serial killer since he was leaving signatures on the bodies and would kill his victims in the exact same manner each time. Every single person in the room was convinced that he would strike again soon if he wasn't caught. Time was of the essence. They had to work as a team and stop him dead in his tracks.

Nina's entire adulthood had been dedicated to becoming an FBI agent. Her career was everything to her. She did not have any sort of a social life. None at all! Her most exciting social events consisted of visiting her parents on a bimonthly basis for a pasta feast. They were part Italian and they loved to make their own pasta on Sunday afternoons after attending church together. Nina loved these afternoons with her beloved parents and with her remaining brother. When the meeting finally adjourned, Jasper turned back to Nina.

"I bet you are hungry. You've had a long day. There's a great steakhouse near here. Could I tempt you to come and grab a bite with me?" Nina's eyes brightened. Now that was her idea of a wonderful offer.

"I'd love that." Jasper offered,

"Are you parked here? If so, we could go in my car. After dinner, I could drive you back to your car?"

"That sounds terrific. Let me make a quick call to my boss and then we can be on our way."

Less than ten minutes later, Jasper and Nina jumped into his 96 Mustang and went to the restaurant. Jasper had called and made a reservation while Nina was on the phone with her boss. The staff was ready for them when they arrived.

An elegant, white table clothed table was awaiting them. Candles were lit and they enjoyed a striking view of the Reno Skyline. Jasper sat across from her. A waiter approached and, without saying a word, poured them a generous portion of wine. He left the bottle for them. Rain drops started to gently hit the window. Nina couldn't help but think how magical it all was. They talked nonstop and laughed. Jasper occasionally touched Nina's arm while he spoke. She had goosebumps. She felt electrified. The room was dark except for the flickering yellow of the candles. The flickers danced and reminded Nina of an arc of brilliant gold in the blackness. She felt mesmerized by Jasper. This was a feeling she had rarely experienced so far in her young life. Jasper watched her intently as she sipped the crimson colored wine. She had already managed to cast a spell on him. This dreamy feeling he was experiencing was not like him. He was generally all business. He was married to his career. Sure, he had a few casual romantic relationships over the years. However, he had never been in love. He never wanted to take his prior relationships to a more serious level. He was about to turn thirty-four. His father often encouraged him to get married and give him grandchildren. As much as he wanted to please him, he always felt that his request was out of the question. His career was so important to him. This beautiful lady in front of him completely caught him off guard. He was in awe of her. Their gazes locked from across the table. They became lost in the depths of each other's eyes. Her powder blue eyes were stunning. Jasper looked longingly at the subtle curve of her neck, the delicate slope of her shoulders. Everything else around them faded away. They barely noticed the waiter as he quietly placed a plate of grapes and cheese in front of them.

They continue to sip their wine. Jasper watched her every move, how she sipped their top shelf wine. Then she delivered a grape to her perfectly shaped lips. She punctured the skin with her teeth. She smiled at Jasper flirtatiously as she crushed the grape and felt the juices exploding into her mouth. Once Nina finished devouring the fruit, Jasper affectionately fed her another one. Time stood still. The rain was getting more intense. It was rhythmically hitting the window next to them. They sat in silence, sipping their wine. Finally, they shared a decadent chocolate mousse for dessert. The concoction was rich and creamy. They shared off of a single spoon and fed each other.

Eventually, it became clear that the wait staff was eager to end their shifts and go home. Jasper and Nina thanked them for their outstanding service. They exited the restaurant and went out into the rain together. Jasper took off his jacket and held it over Nina so she wouldn't get drenched. They giggled and inevitably waded through puddles. Thunder and lightning boomed directly above them. The eye of the storm was close by. Jasper quickly opened the car door and gently guided Nina into the front passenger seat.

They drove back to the Reno Police Department. Jasper spotted Nina's rental car and pulled up next to it.

"Tonight was amazing. I felt more relaxed than I have in a long time. Will you be at the meeting tomorrow morning?" Jasper inquired.

"I sure will be. I can't believe that it is already one in the morning Virginia time. I loved our evening together. Thank you for everything." Jasper pulled Nina close. She tasted his soft lips. They still had a hint of the whiskey which he had just indulged in moments before. His kisses became harder and deeper. She felt the rush of helplessness beginning to set in. Jasper's insistent mouth was parting her shaking lips. She felt such intense sensations, feelings she never knew she was capable of. Soft tremors hijacked her body. Finally, Nina had the self control to bid Jasper goodnight. She knew that if she stayed a moment longer, she might do things she would end up regretting.He walked her protectively to her rental car. His longing for her was unmistakable.

"Please text me once you get to the hotel," Jasper pleaded. "I want to make sure you are safe. There have been way too many sketchy things going on around here lately," Nina promised and exited the parking lot. She went directly to her hotel. She checked in. The customer service at the front desk was impeccable. They were friendly and went out of their way to make her feel welcome.

Finally, she took the elevator up to the fifth level. She entered her room. It was immaculate. The room was bathed in the hues of nature, forest greens, powder whites and earthy browns. The decor soothed Nina and gave her the sense of being in a home away from home. It was warm and cheerful. The ceiling was vaulted. The heater was working over time. Nina started to perspire. She saw a Reno Gazette newspaper placed on the coffee table. Nina sighed. It had been a very long day. It felt like she had left Quantico days ago even though she knew it was not even twenty-four hours yet since her departure. She hung her clothes up on the hangers and stripped down completely out of her stiff, starched feeling suit. She turned the shower on to a tepid temperature. Once steam enveloped the room, she lowered herself into the water. It felt like pure heaven. Every muscle in her body ached. She used the lavender soap provided by the hotel. The soap was rich, calming and luxurious. The non relenting stream of water pelted her scalp. Nina normally rushed in the shower. Tonight she took her time and lingered She needed the extra time to relax. Finally, she turned off the water and snuggled into a large, terry cloth robe. She went into the bedroom area and checked her phone. A text from Jasper had been delivered while she had been in the shower. She smiled.

"Hey, beautiful. I loved tonight more than I can say. I hope the night goes by quickly so I can see you again." Nina's heart pounded with excitement. She was normally not so taken by anyone, but Jasper intrigued her to the highest level. He had cast a spell on her.

32

Wyatt's back ached. His shift at the cemetery had just started and he already felt exhausted. What made it even worse was that he was consumed with jealousy. Luke texted him that he was going to take Cosette to the lake house. His heart ached. His stomach had a pit in it. Here he was, moping around in the town cemetery, while his cousin was spending days at a romantic lake house with the woman of his dreams. Life just sucked! He needed to do something. He felt as if he would end up completely losing his mind if he didn't make Cosette his very soon. So far, his plan had not been effective.

"I've made zero progress,"he thought glumly. He needed her. He felt like Luke was getting closer to her by the day.Then he concocted a wonderful idea. He reached for his cell and texted Luke.

"Hey, cuz, Hope you guys are having a blast. I work tonight-all night. I'll need to sleep for a few hours after my shift. How 'bout I come hang out with you tomorrow around 11:00 a.m. at the lake house? I'll bring lunch?" His pulse quickened and his face broke into a smile. This was the first smile he had experienced in days. "Maybe there was hope after all?"

His loyal cousin texted back fifteen minutes later. It was a done deal. Wyatt was expected there tomorrow for lunch and sailing. He had just a handful of hours to figure out all the details of his strategy.

The following morning, the conference room was again filled with law enforcement at the Reno Police Department. They agreed to meet there rather than at the Virginia City station because the conference rooms accommodated more people. Jasper was the first person to arrive. He was on pins and needles to see Nina. Dr. Johnson, the Forensic Psychologist, arrived next. Then the attractive Nina sauntered in. She took Jasper's breath away. The chief of police and three more detectives arrived next. They all huddled around the solidly built conference table. The chief spoke first.

"Good morning! Thank you all for being here so promptly. We have a long day ahead of us. Please help yourselves to coffee, tea and donuts located on the table at the back corner of the room. Some of the preliminary forensic reports from Harper Metcalf's homicide have come back. We may finally have our first piece of evidence. A business card was found under Harper's body. It appears that the killer more than likely dropped it by accident." The chief projected an image of the card on the overhead digital projector. It was a plain, white business card from "Bayside South San Francisco BMW" It then stated the address and phone number in smaller print below the name of the business. The card was a general card for the business rather than a card for a specific salesperson. No fingerprints were found on the card. The chief continued, "Nina, I'd appreciate it if you could head to South San Francisco after this meeting. We have already reserved a room for you at the nearby Hilton Hotel. Please go to the dealership and question anyone and everyone who is on shift there. Try to get them to show you documents of all recent test drives and sales. We technically need a search warrant for that but these type of businesses tend to be cooperative with law enforcement."

Jasper felt utterly disappointed. They were sending Nina out of town already? Nina felt dismayed as well. They had already planned on having dinner together after the meeting. They both had a hard time concentrating on the remainder of the meeting. Nina felt Jasper's foot gently touch her lower calf. She looked over at him. She felt electricity and excitement radiate throughout her body. Jasper noticed that his hands were clammy. His pulse was racing. He was developing feelings for her at a record breaking pace. The feeling of helplessness scared him.The chief continued,

"I have been doing a lot of research and I think we need to investigate another angle in these string of murders as well. There is a satanic cult just sixteen miles away from Virginia City. An inside source reported to me that this cult, "Hell's Destiny," has been discussing sacrifices they have recently committed. We can't afford to dismiss that they may be involved in the recent murders in our area. Detective Alexander, I need you to contact Detective Bethany French. She is based in Carson City. I can give you her contact information after the meeting. She has been monitoring their activity for months already. Plus, she may be able to give you more feedback as to whether these homicides could be connected to this cult. She tends to be a wealth of information when it comes to occult activity."

"Consider it done, Chief. I will pay Bethany a visit as soon as our meeting is adjourned." The chief continued to go over the few forensic reports which had already been processed. Other than the business card, there was nothing telling left at the scenes. No fingerprints, fibers or the murderer's DNA. Law enforcement was perplexed by this difficult case. They were convinced that someone highly experienced and organized was committing the homicides.

The meeting ended. Jasper walked Nina out to her car. He was nervously fidgeting. Nina could sense that he wanted to tell her something. Once they got to her car, Jasper hesitantly asked if he may accompany her to South San Francisco.

"My schedule is pretty clear until tomorrow afternoon. Any business I need to take care of can be easily handled on my laptop," he insisted. Nina couldn't contain her excitement,

"I'd love that." They agreed to drive in Jasper's patrol car. They swung by Nina's hotel and she packed an overnight bag to bring with her. Then they drove to Virginia City to pick up a change of clothing for Jasper. They estimated they would be there in under four hours. They got onto Highway 80. The conversation was natural and ever flowing. The hours flew by. They stopped for lunch at a diner near a rest stop along the way. They both ordered burgers and fries. After dining, they got back into the car and went straight to their destination.

Once they arrived in the Bay Area, Jasper made a suggestion.

"We can't check into the hotel until 3:00 p.m. Why don't we go look at some tourist sites before we go back to the room. I figure we will go to the dealership first thing tomorrow morning."

"I love the sound of that," Nina giggled excitedly. From the distance, they spotted it, the world famous Golden Gate Bridge. The iconic suspension bridge was awe inspiring. It stretched over the San Francisco Bay from Marin County to the city of San Francisco. Its well known International Orange color glistened in the afternoon sun. Nina snapped countless photos. She had only visited The City by the Bay one time several years ago.

The next stop was Pier 39. Parking was not an easy endeavor but finally Jasper found a nearby garage which still had a handful of vacant spots. The pier stretched into the choppy bay. The distinct smell of sea salt was tantalizing to the couple. Pier 39 was littered with countless trendy shops and restaurants, even a video arcade, all catering to the nonstop onslaught of tourists. Nina pointed to a festive two story carousel. It was the pier's most dominant feature. Children and parents alike looked delighted as they twirled in circles on their horses, hippos and ostriches. Boats sailed in the bay, underneath the Golden Gate Bridge and even around Alcatraz. Nina and Jasper continued to walk and explore the pier. The couple followed the persistent, boisterous barking they kept hearing. They discovered at least a dozen sea lions perched on a nearby dock. Nina was delighted. She always had a special place in her heart for all kinds of animals.This group of sea lions were particularly endearing to Nina. Their shenanigans were entertaining. They were lounging in the dazzling afternoon sun. Some were piled on top of each other. They were large in size. Nina estimated that some of them weighed about eight hundred pounds.

The next stop was Ghirardelli Square. It was a short walk from the pier. It was a public square with shops, restaurants and ritzy galleries. From this location and Pier 39, they were also able to enjoy spectacular views of the Golden Gate Bridge and Alcatraz. Jasper reminded Nina that the chocolate here was known to be some of the very best in the United States. They stopped at the Original Ghirardelli Ice Cream and Chocolate Shop. Nina had a serious addiction to sweets. Somehow she still managed to maintain her enviable physique, probably due to a combination of excellent genetics teamed with all of the exercise she got both from her job and during her free time. They feasted on chocolate, confections, sundaes and even hot cocoa. The timing of the hot cocoa was perfect. The fog started to lazily roll in. Nina was shivering. The surrounding trees were veiled in the lightest of mists. The fog made the city appear blurred like an old paining.

"Shall we head back to the car?" Jasper gently inquired.

"Yes, we shall," responded Nina enthusiastically. Nina looped her arm through his and they made their way back to the garage. The fog was beginning to get thicker. They could only see a few feet in front of them. Jasper took off his sweatshirt. After some polite resistance on Nina's part, she caved in and allowed him to wrap her in the fuzzy, thermal garment. She snuggled closer to him, relishing his body heat. The fog was a ghost grey color. It was mirage like as it moved noiselessly over cars and fire hydrants. It appeared filmy and lifelike.They sought shelter in the patrol car. Jasper quickly turned on the heat. He punched the Hilton Hotel's address into his GPS. The duo exited the parking garage and entered into a great deal of traffic.

"This is another reason I love living in Virginia City. The traffic isn't bad. I have always been more of a country boy. I love visiting cities but I prefer small towns when it comes to a permanent residency." Nina responded,

"I feel the same way. I am a country girl at heart. I love being an FBI agent but the job generally forces me to live in larger cities." Nina felt so comfortable with Jasper that she told him how her younger sister was killed by a serial killer. "That is the main reason that I became an agent. I wanted to dedicate my life to capturing these monsters. I don't want other people to go through the hell that my family and I went through when my sister was brutally taken away from us." Jasper was a great listener. He was soothing and supportive. There wasn't anything about this man that didn't fascinate her. She hated to admit this, even to herself, but she was crazy about him. This was unlike her. She always kept her distance from men in the past. She was casual with other men. She never wanted to commit and always felt lukewarm towards them. He ignited a passion and excitement in her that she never knew was possible. The passion combined with the deep comfort she felt with him, was enough to make her never want to say goodbye to him. Her intense and sudden feelings scared her.

On the way to the hotel, they experienced a rare silence. Nina was in her own world, dreaming about the incredible man next to her. Jasper was, at least, equally enamored with Nina, if not more. She made his head spin.

"This incredible woman has me under the spell of all spells." Jasper melted at the thought that he was about to spend the night with her. His dream was to hold her in his arms all night long. He needed her like lungs need air. Nina reached over and gently held Jasper's hand. He squeezed her hand back. They both felt an indescribable happiness yet they were anxious knowing they were about to spend their first night together.

They entered the hotel and noticed the floral aroma wafting from the expansive courtyard. They went to the check in counter. A stout, business like brunette with a chin length bob haircut greeted them. She pointed to their electronic key card envelope and indicated to them what their room number was.

"Enjoy your stay and please do not hesitate to let us know if we can do anything to make your stay more comfortable." They took the elevator up to the 8th floor in awkward silence. Jasper slid the key into the card slot. As soon as the door opened, the couple entered. Jasper passionately yet gently pushed Nina against the wall. His body pressed into her. He kissed her, hard and deep. Nina's arms pulled Jasper even closer to her. She stroked her fingers through his hair. His strong, rough hands ignited her with an intense passion.

Just then, Nina's cell obnoxiously blared and disturbed their moment. Nina saw that it was a call from her mother.

"I'm so sorry, Jasper. I need to pick this up." Nina answered the call and could hear her mother softly crying. Nina felt an instant sense of dread.

"Mom, are you ok?"

"No, I'm not. Your grandmother died. She had a stroke a few hours ago." Nina could feel her heart breaking. Her grandmother was like a second mother to her. She was so warm, kind and she was always there for her. She felt a deep sadness. They spoke a few more minutes and then Nina went over to the bed and collapsed on it. She huddled into a ball and cried. Jasper held her and tried to comfort her. Her body shuddered as she wailed. Rather than sharing a night of passion, Jasper tenderly held the grieving Nina. After hours of cuddling and talking with him, she began to calm down. She had never felt so close to another person in her entire life. His feelings for her were definitely mutual.

33

Detective Alexander contacted Detective French after the meeting. The latter invited Kelly to meet her at the police station in Carson City. Kelly prepared the files she was going to share with the cult expert.

Detective French was waiting for her in a conference room by the time she arrived. The detective greeted Kelly enthusiastically and with a lot of warmth.

"Good afternoon, Detective Alexander. Please call me Bethany. I am eager to look over the specific details of the recent homicides."

"It's a pleasure to meet you, Bethany. Please call me Kelly. I am looking forward to our meeting too. We are trying to not leave a stone unturned in these cases. I hear you are quite an expert when it comes to the occult." Bethany blushed at Kelly's compliment.

"Aw, thank you. I have definitely developed a fascination for it. There is quite a bit of cult activity in this area. May I see what you brought?" The ladies sat at the table and sprawled out all the forensic photos and documents complete with dates, approximate times of death and unique features found at the scenes.

Bethany spent some time quietly poring over the information. Kelly could see that she was thoughtful and meticulous. She kept referring to her own laptop and inputting the dates of the murders. She finally spoke,

"Based on the dates of the three murders, I find it very unlikely that a Satanic cult is involved.These cults tend to follow very detailed plans for their murders. Their sacrifices are connected to the phases of the moon. They generally kill under the light of the full moon.

Satanists have a flurry of activities, especially with the start of the Harvest Full Moon. The two weeks following the Harvest Full Moon is filled with ways to build terror. In fact, farmers in the area know to be extra cautious with their livestock, in particularly goats, during nights with a full moon. The climax of terror occurs on Halloween night. Also, their sacrifices are usually performed in nature such as a mountain top or a forest. These three homicide victims were all killed within the confines of a home or a building."

Kelly was grateful for Bethany's feedback. As she left the station, she felt confident that they could scratch Satanic cult members as people of interest off of their list.

Wyatt called ahead to the Dragon Pond, his favorite restaurant in Tahoe City. His goal was to impress and please Cosette. He practically ordered half the menu, pot stickers, spring rolls, crab puffs, moo shu pork, sweet and sour pork, fried rice and even chicken chow mein. They would be well fed today. His mouth watered after he picked up the food and continued on to

Rubicon. He turned down the long driveway and punched in the code. He rang at the doorbell. Cosette opened the door and greeted him warmly. He had to hold back a gasp. She looked even more ravishing than ever. The Tahoe sun had been good to her. She looked much more relaxed than normal. Her perfect skin had a golden tone to it. She wore a trendy, aqua colored swim cover. Her hair was thrown up into a high pony tail.

"Wyatt, we are so excited for your visit. Come on in," Cosette gushed. To Wyatt's dismay, his cousin was immediately by her side.

"Hey, buddy. I'm so glad you could make it. The food smells incredible. Why don't we have an early lunch on the back deck. After, we can go sailing on Emerald Bay." Wyatt feigned enthusiasm. What he really wanted was to get rid of Luke and have Cosette all to himself. He reminded himself that this was the final stretch. He just needed to be meticulous with his plan and be patient. He was proud of himself for concocting such a brilliant idea. Anything to get the woman of his dreams all for himself. She was well worth the wait.

They went onto the deck and set up the various containers in a serve yourself buffet style. They opened a red wine and feasted. Wyatt continuously filled Luke's wine glass in hopes of getting him intoxicated. Wyatt's plan would be much easier to fulfill if Luke was at least somewhat tipsy. Cosette was sitting way too close to Luke for Wyatt's liking. It made him crazy with jealousy and sick to his stomach. Everything he feared would happen, had obviously materialized. It was evident that the duo was closer than ever. They could barely keep their eyes off of each other. Wyatt hated to admit it to himself, but they looked deeply in love.

After lunch, Luke brought them down to the impressive sailboat. The sail stood proud. It was painted a glossy turquoise color. Wyatt had been certain that Luke would suggest an afternoon sail. This piece was key to his scheme. They were off on their adventure. The sail rose higher and higher. It cast a dark shadow down the boat ramp. They exited the sleepy lagoon connected to Luke's property and headed towards the beckoning horizon. The sky was cloudless. The sail calmly swayed from side to side. They were gradually moving away from the safety of the shore. The water appeared mirror like. The hull creaked and moaned with each gust of wind. The bay was forested with sailing masts. They passed waterfront bars and restaurants. Jet skiers and speedboats raced passed them. From a distance, they could see how the waves crashed onto the rocky shoreline. The wind was starting to pick up as they ventured further out into the lake. The sun glinted on the now choppy water. Cosette announced that she would go down into the cabin to make a pitcher of margaritas. Luke and Wyatt were grateful for her offer.

Wyatt worked the main sail. Luke started to tighten the boom vang. With an unexpected gust of wind, the boom swung out and hit him. He flew over the lifeline and into the water. Wyatt pretended he did not witness the horrible incident. The boat continued to sail forward at a record speed. Wyatt's face broke out into a satisfied smile, as he realized that this fortunate fluke would not leave the blood on his hands. After a few minutes, he went down to the cabin to see if Cosette needed any help with the refreshments.

"Thank you for offering. I actually have it prepared along with a cheese and cracker platter. Shall we head up and start the party?" Wyatt hesitantly agreed. He wanted to stall as long as possible before Cosette realized that Luke was no longer on the watercraft.They went up on deck and Cosette called out Luke's name. Panic begin to rise within her when he failed to respond. Wyatt continued with his innocent act and began to call out for him too. He feigned a fearful look on his face.

"Where is Luke?" Cosette screamed. They searched the deck but he clearly was no longer on the boat. Wyatt went to channel sixteen and in a commanding tone barked,

"Mayday! Mayday! Man overboard!" Cosette felt her limbs getting weak. How could this happen? She knew that Luke was skilled with sailing. He had sailed since he was a young boy. Wyatt pulled Cosette into his arms and comforted her. Cosette was too distraught to notice that his behavior was more typical of a lover than as a family friend. He held her tight. It felt so right to him. She belonged with him.

"What if he drowns? I won't be able to survive without him," she sobbed frantically. Her comment was like a knife in Wyatt's heart. He tried to calm his racing mind. He reminded himself that in the end this was for the best. She would get over Luke and they would spend their lives together. They were soulmates. He had no doubt in his mind about it. She belonged with him. He worshipped the very ground she walked on.

He took out his binoculars and pretended he was searching for Luke.

Suddenly, to Wyatt's horror, he detected commotion in the distance. Cosette emerged from her cocoon of grief and went to look. They both saw Luke being pulled up onto a twenty-seven foot vessel. It was a boat from the Marine Unit. Wyatt knew that they were responsible for rescue activities on numerous waterways in the county. Their area included Emerald Bay. They pulled him out of the frigid water and began administering life saving measures. The water temperature, at this depth, was about fifty-five

degrees. Luke showed clear signs of
hypothermia. They immediately wrapped him in a
few warm blankets. He was shivering
uncontrollably. His speech was slurred and his
hands were fumbling. He appeared confused.
His pulse was irregular. Luke was raced to the
Incline Village Community Hospital.

Cosette was besides herself with grief and
worry. Of course, Wyatt had no choice but to look
concerned and offer to take her to the hospital.
They drove to the hospital enshrouded in more
silence than his solo shifts at the cemetery.
Cosette was ghostlike in appearance. Her skin
was so pale that it was virtually see through. The
medical staff members were attempting to
stabilize Luke by the time they arrived. They
were tight lipped and they refrained from giving
any further information. Cosette felt like she was
about to climb the walls. Her anxiety was at an
all time high. Wyatt guided Cosette to seats in
the corner of the waiting area. He wrapped his
arm around her delicate shoulders and pulled her
closer to him. She began to cry again. He rolled
his eyes as she wept but luckily for him, this

gesture was not seen by anyone. He felt agitated by her obvious love for his cousin.

"Nothing I can't correct," he reminded himself reassuringly. At least an hour and a half passed. Finally, a physician came out to the almost empty waiting area. Cosette was on pins and needles for the update on Luke's health. The doctor was calm and optimistic. He looked at Wyatt.

"You are a family member of Luke Meier's?

"Yes, I am his cousin. How is he doing?"

"He is improving dramatically. We were able to treat his hypothermia. He does have a moderate concussion from when he was hit on the head. For that reason, I would feel better keeping him overnight in the hospital for observation." Cosette let out a great sigh of relief.

"That is the best news I have heard in a long time. May I see him?"

"Yes, we just transferred him to his private room. He has been checked in." Cosette's eyes lit up with relief and happiness.

"Thank you so much, doctor."

Wyatt and Cosette took the stairs up to the second level. Cosette could barely contain her excitement. She practically ran to his room. Once she spotted his room number, she burst into the room. Luke looked tired and pale but his eyes lit up when he saw Cosette.

"I'm so glad you are here!" Luke reached his hand out for Cosette. She pulled up a chair and sat as close to him as possible. Wyatt stood awkwardly in the corner. He felt left out and excluded.

"I've been so worried about you, Luke." Cosette's eyes began to tear up. "I was so scared." Wyatt noticed how touched Luke was by Cosette's words. He wanted to throw up. Jealousy consumed him. They visited for a while. After a bit, Luke could barely keep his eyes open any more.

"Why don't you both go back to the lake house. I'll rest up and be back to you before you know it." Cosette seemed hesitant but she could see how exhausted Luke looked. She didn't want to intrude any longer. She reluctantly agreed. Wyatt walked her out to his car and drove her back to the lake house. Cosette was once again completely silent. Wyatt played some music to try to make the awkward silence less obvious.

34

Once they arrived at Luke's lake house, Cosette offered to heat up their Chinese leftovers. Wyatt thanked her for her kindness. He headed out to the deck and prepared for their meal. He popped a bottle of bubbly and lit candles. There was a blanket of sparkling stars in the endless sky overhead.In certain areas in the sky, the stars looked like scattered moon dust. The night sky was such a welcome sight for him. It felt magical and tranquil. He gazed heavenward and prayed that he would finally be able to break through and get closer to Cosette tonight. This was his chance. They were all alone for once. Usually his pesky cousin was all over her but not tonight. He could hear the waves gently lapping against the dock and shoreline. The sound of a motorboat purred in the distance. As he could see Cosette completing the final preparations of their meal, he went inside to help her carry the various dishes. They sat at the candle encircled table. The evening was pleasant. Finally, the conversation was flowing smoothly. He made a point of regularly filling her champagne glass. He ensured that it was bottomless. He could see that she was feeling the effects of the alcohol. She seemed more serene than she had been earlier.

Cosette was indeed feeling much better. The relief she felt that Luke was on the mend was overwhelming. She was counting the minutes to be able to pick him up from the hospital tomorrow. She already missed him so much. She hated being away from him. It was torture. Fatigue was starting to wear her down. It had been such a long and stressful day. She could hardly wait to go upstairs to her bedroom and fall into a blissful slumber. She was aware that she needed to still stay and talk to Wyatt for a while. He had been so kind and comforting to her through this entire fiasco. He was a good man. It made Cosette happy to know that Luke had such a dear friend in his cousin. They continued to talk. Then,Wyatt said something which hurt Cosette to the deepest level. He began to talk about Luke's ex fiancee, Eden.

"He really loved Eden," Wyatt stated confidently. All Cosette could weakly mutter was:

"Oh? That isn't the impression he gave me."

"He is a typical man. It is an ego thing. He was out of his mind in love with her. In fact, I have no doubt that he still is."

Cosette fought back tears but managed to say,

"But he told me he only loved her as a friend and that's why he called off their short engagement." Wyatt laughed,

"Is that what he told you? That dog! That isn't how it went at all. Eden lost interest in him. She was running around with half the men in town. It destroyed Luke.Then another man got her pregnant. Luke threw a huge fit and insisted she get an abortion. He was on the verge of losing his mind because of his extreme jealousy. Eden threw the engagement ring at his face and dumped him. He's still in love with her. I am convinced. There is no other way." Cosette was startled and felt as if she had just been punched in the stomach. Luke always seemed so truthful to her but this was an entirely different version Wyatt was telling her. She was speechless.

35

Eden was sitting with her best friend, Samantha, at the Watering Trough when she heard the news. Austin came over and told them that Luke had a terrible boating accident. He told them the details. It took every ounce of self control to hold it together and not to collapse into a sobbing heap. Of course, she was beyond relieved that he was now recuperating in the hospital. She had a secret that not even her very best friend or her mother were privy to. She was still hopelessly in love with Luke Meier. He was the love of her life. The time she spent being his girlfriend and then, for a brief period, his fiancee, was her definition of heaven. During that time period, she had been walking on air, day and night. That was, until he left her. Sure, he was a gentleman about it but the grief she felt was earth shattering. They say time is supposed to heal all pain. Well, she was still waiting for her time of healing to begin. He made it crystal clear to her that he loved her as a friend but he did not have a romantic interest in her. There was nothing in the world she could do to change his mind. Eden knew that she was an extremely beautiful woman. That clearly wasn't enough to win his love. In the past several months, she had seen him countless times with that flight attendant. He had a look in his eyes when he gazed at this other woman. It was a look of pure adoration. A look he never once had when he laid his eyes on Eden. She stared moodily down at the melting ice in her cocktail.

Nina finally fell asleep at about four in the morning. Jasper held her close to him the entire time. Eventually, he nodded off and he was able to sleep for about two hours. Nina woke up with very puffy eyelids.

"It sure isn't going to look very professional for me to show up at the dealership looking like this." Jasper had an idea and said he would be right back. He went to the ice machine and brought a bucket full of cubes to Nina. She was very grateful and she was touched by his thoughtfulness. He had been so patient and supportive with her. They were expecting to enjoy a night of intimacy together but the tragic news of her grandmother's passing, derailed everything. They shared a different type of intimacy instead, emotional intimacy. He held her and comforted her all night. She told him memories of her grandmother until the early morning hours. The ice helped to reduce the puffiness. Finally, she looked as good as new.

They arrived at the BMW dealership just after 10:00 a.m. and were greeted by two salespeople. She showed them her FBI badge. They both seemed taken aback. She asked if she could speak to the manager. A gentleman in his mid 50s came out into the reception area minutes later. He was clean cut and sported salt and pepper hair. His eyes were lively and hazel in color. His complexion was similar to the color of wheat.

"Good morning. I'm Richard Kraft. How may I help you today?" Nina discreetly flashed her badge to him and he then promptly escorted both Nina and Jasper back to his office. Without giving too many details, Nina explained to him that she was investigating a few homicides in the Virginia City area.

"And how does that tie in to my dealership?" He nervously bit his already chapped lower lip.

"There was a business card found at the most recent murder scene. The business card stated your business and address." Nina produced the image of the actual business card found at the crime scene and displayed it to Mr. Kraft.

"I noticed that this card is an exact match to the design and font of your current business card. How long have you had this style of card?"

Mr. Kraft thought for a moment and then stated that they had this version of the exact business card for over two years now.

"I see," Nina responded. "Would it be possible to see your sales records and test drive sign in sheets since the date this type of card was used by your business?" Nina held her breath. She knew he could easily make it difficult and refuse to hand over the information without a warrant. To her relief, he indicated that it would not be a problem.

"The sales records will be more accurate than the test drive records, however. It is not uncommon for groups of friends to come in and test drive together. We only require identification from the individual driving the vehicle. I will give you records from both the sales and the test drives." Nina acknowledged,

"Yes, that is understandable and I appreciate your cooperation. We will take that all into consideration."

A half hour later, Nina and Jasper left with stacks of paperwork. They decided begrudgingly that it was time to head back to Reno.

"I can peruse all the names once I get back to the station," Nina said

36

Wyatt could tell how upset Cosette was. He hoped he hadn't pushed it too far with her. She looked completely crestfallen. She stood up from her seat wearily and weakly announced that she was very tired and needed to go to sleep.

"Of course!" Wyatt responded, feigning enthusiasm in his voice. "Now if you need anything, anything at all, I will be right down the hall from you." Cosette politely thanked him and climbed the stairs to her room. Once inside, she went onto her bed and cried softly. This day was supposed to be wonderful. Instead it was a nightmare from start to finish. Fatigue overtook her and she drifted into a fitful slumber. Wyatt went into his room. He stripped down and got into the shower. He used his favorite men's body wash. He had been told several times that it was a very sexy scent. He needed to be irresistible tonight. He sudsed up and let the stress of the day melt away. Showering had always served as a type of meditation for him. It elevated his mood almost instantly and calmed him.

"Too bad Cosette isn't here to join me...yet anyway." He smiled mischievously.

He dried off and admired his well toned physique in the full length mirror. He needed his washboard abs and muscular, broad chest to do the trick tonight. Then he slipped into a crisp, burgundy colored t-shirt and checkered boxer shorts. He sat on the edge of his bed for a while weighing the pros and cons of what he was about to do. If his seduction worked with Cosette, he would be the happiest man on the planet. If it didn't work, however, he risked losing her forever. He started to lose his confidence. Had she ever even really flirted with him? Had she shown interest for anyone but his damned cousin? No! But how often would he have this opportunity. He was all alone with his obsession for the night. He would be a fool to pass it up. Wyatt entered the hallway and was able to see, thanks to the moonlight shining through the skylight. He opened Cosette's door soundlessly.

"Thank God his cousin had OCD about maintenance in the house. No door creaks in Luke's homes." He could hear Cosette's soft and rhythmical breathing. He edged closer to the bed. The blackout curtains in this room made it difficult to even see his own hand in front of his eyes. He allowed time for his vision to adjust.

Finally he could see her outline. She was definitely sleeping. She was curled comfortably in a fetal position. He didn't have the heart to wake her up.

"True love isn't selfish. She has just had a very long and stressful day. Let her sleep some more still. What's the rush. We have the rest of our lives to spend together," Wyatt thought happily. He gently crept in under the sheets on the other side of the bed. He could feel her body heat. This was the closest Wyatt had gotten to her yet. It felt intoxicating. Cosette made his head spin and his blood boil. She was everything he ever wanted in a wife and then some. He was wide eyed and excited. He couldn't fall asleep knowing she was so close to him. This continued for a number of hours. Finally she stirred. Wyatt gazed lovingly at her face. She opened her eyes and seemed momentarily confused and still half asleep.She sat up appearing panicked and disoriented.

"Wyatt? What are you doing here?" Cosette's voice sounded agitated and alarmed.

"I was just checking in on you to make sure you are doing ok," Wyatt lamely stated.

"You needed to come into my bed for that?" She jumped out of bed and quickly threw on the robe she had placed on the nearby chair the night before. Cosette felt mortified by Wyatt's visit. She tried to calm herself down. His behavior was highly inappropriate. This was a disaster. She knew how close he was to Luke. Cosette continued, "I need to freshen up and change. I can meet you down for breakfast in a little while? She tried to keep her voice calm and even.

"I really need to talk to you," pleaded Wyatt.

"That is fine but I would feel more comfortable having a conversation when I meet you down at the dining table in about a half hour," insisted Cosette. Wyatt knew that being persistent at this point would only push her further away. She did not have the response he was hoping for. He was crushed but he tried to mask his disappointment.

"Of course, I will see you downstairs after you get ready." He left her room with his head down. He went downstairs and brewed coffee. Then he made waffles for breakfast. His hands were fumbling nervously. He washed and prepared the various berries. Wyatt was fighting back tears. He rapidly calculated what he would say to her when she came downstairs.

As soon as Cosette could tell that Wyatt had descended down the stairs, she quietly locked her bedroom door. She could hardly wait to go pick Luke up at the hospital. She showered and got dressed. Her heart was pounding. She felt anxious about Wyatt's unwanted visit to her room.

"What was he thinking and what did he want to tell me?" She wished that she could stay locked in her room until the time came that Luke was discharged from the hospital.

Cosette forced herself to go downstairs. She had promised him she would talk to him. She was a woman of her word. She entered the dining area. Wyatt looked embarrassed. He had set out the breakfast dishes and poured the coffee. Cosette sat down and looked up at him.

"I feel we really need to talk, Cosette." She looked up at him silently. Dread filled her. "I need to explain my actions. I have known you for several months now." He hesitated and looked down. Cosette waited for him to continue. "I feel that we have a strong connection. We really click together well. I am not a sixteen year old boy with stars in my eyes. I have lived long enough by now to know when something is real." Cosette did not like where this conversation was heading. She clearly did not share his feelings. "I would love nothing more than to be in a committed relationship with you." Cosette felt tongue tied. She knew that she needed to handle this situation as delicately as possible. She couldn't admit that she loved Luke since Luke was not even aware of her feelings yet." Wyatt moved his

chair closer to her and grasped her hand.
Cosette replied hesitantly,

"I am very flattered, Wyatt. You are a great
man."His face dropped. He couldn't conceal his
disappointment. Cosette continued, "I am just not
in a place right now to even think about
embarking on a romantic relationship. My divorce
isn't final yet. Right now, my primary focus is to
get my son here. I feel lost without Spencer. As
you know, there has been a delay with that
because of the recent murders."

"Of course, Cosette. I understand." Wyatt
began to feel a shred of hope from her words. He
just needed to be patient. She was worth it. Soon
she would be more settled in town and then he
would try again. He purposely changed the
subject in hopes of making them both feel more
at ease.

37

Nina pored over all the documents from the car dealership. She was sorting through thousands of names and addresses. She had a special app which pinpointed anyone with an address in the state of Nevada. The computer fixated on one entry in particular. A buyer of a M5 BMW. The car was purchased approximately three months ago. The gentleman lived in Virginia City. It was Wyatt Meier! Nina began researching information about him online. His employment records indicated that he was the caretaker at the cemetery in Virginia City. He was single and no offspring were listed. Jasper would know more about him. Wyatt was born and raised there. Jasper was too. He must have additional information she could collect about Wyatt before she paid him a visit. She texted Jasper. He was still in the area. He would be there in a few minutes. She could hardly wait to pick his brain about Wyatt.

As promised, Jasper arrived at the station shortly after. Nina thanked him for meeting her on such short notice. They went into one of the smaller conference rooms.

"Nina, I am on pins and needles about what you discovered. Do tell."

"Well, the computer picked up a Virginia City resident who was a client at the BMW dealership a few months back. He purchased an M5."

"Wyatt?" Jasper blurted out before Nina could even give him the name. She was startled by his quick response. "It's a small town. I practically grew up with him. It is hard not to notice when one of your best buddies cruises into town with a car like that. I didn't realize he bought it from the dealership in question though."

"I am going to set up a time to interview him," Nina continued. "Is there any way you could sit in on the interview? He may be more open and relaxed if you are there."

"There sure is a way you can convince me. Have dinner with me tomorrow night?" Nina felt a wave of happiness by his invitation.

"I would love that."

The call Cosette had been waiting for finally arrived. It was time to pick up Luke from the hospital. She had gotten to the point where she couldn't bear to not be by his side. Wyatt drove Cosette to pick up Luke. Their conversation in the car felt strained and uncomfortable to Cosette. Relief washed over her as they arrived and saw Luke. Cosette couldn't help but to race into his arms. He held her closely. Wyatt was irked by their obvious affection for each other.

Once they arrived back at the lake house, Wyatt awkwardly announced that it was time for him to return to Virginia City. Upon his departure, the couple went out onto the deck. It was a glorious day. They both felt elated to be reunited with one another. They sat closely together and looked out over the peaceful lake. At the moment, the water appeared glass like. Its color was a combination of turquoise and shimmering blues. Seagulls dive bombed into its watery depths. The snow-topped mountain peaks looked majestic in the distance. Kayakers passed by. The boaters were in a festive mood. Their laughter echoed onto the beach. The air was fresh. Cosette could detect her favorite scent coming over from the neighbor's back yard, freshly cut lawn. The sweet aroma of nearby flowers overpowered her senses. The sky was spotted with an occasional fluffy cloud. A distant airplane left streaks in the sky. Cosette decided not to mention Wyatt's overtures to Luke. What was the point? After all, Cosette and Luke were still not in any kind of romantic relationship. Plus, it could strain the relationship between the cousins. That is the last thing she wanted to do. Luke's mood suddenly seemed serious.

"I have a surprise for you, Cosette. I was hesitant to set it up it without checking with you first." Cosette held her breath in anticipation. Luke continued, "I have arranged for your son to come here in two days. I know you miss him terribly but you are hesitant for him to come here because of the recent murders. With your permission, he will land in Reno. Your mother will accompany him on the flight. We will pick them up at the airport and bring them here, to the lake house. Your mom offered to stay as long as you'd like her to. I figured they will be safe here since we are quite a distance from where the murders took place. Plus, your leave of absence from the airline is almost over. Your mother said she would be delighted to watch Spencer when you are out of town." Cosette was speechless. This was the best news she had heard in a long time. She had missed Spencer constantly. To think that in about forty-eight hours, she would be able to hold him again was enough to bring tears of joy to her eyes.

"Oh, Luke. I will never be able to tell you what this surprise means to me. I agree with you. I feel they will be completely safe as long as they stay at the lake house. Thank you so much from the bottom of my heart." They embraced. Luke pulled her close. Neither one of them wanted to let go.

38

Eden woke up in her semi dark room. Grief engulfed her. She immediately became bombarded with thoughts of Luke. Thoughts of him had been haunting her every morning for a long time. He had been living in her broken heart, rent free, for more years than she cared to count. Her vision came softly into focus. Eden felt lethargic and somber. She had just endured a restless night. She rarely enjoyed a solid, restful night of sleep.

"Stop feeling sorry for yourself. You have a long, packed day ahead of you. Get up, go for a walk. Snap out of it, Eden," she berated herself.

Eden waded through the semi darkness and prepared herself for a long walk. She poured herself a steaming cup of black coffee. She winced at the bitter taste of it. The coffee was extra strong today. Just what she needed.

She exited through her front door and realized that she was just in time to see the glorious sunrise. Long strips of reds, yellows and oranges streaked across the pale blue sky. The rising sun cast a rosy hue on the surrounding desert. The sky was littered with crimson and amber tinted clouds. From a distance, lightning and thunder raged with fury. A bolt of lightning tore across the sky. Thunder clapped and startled her. The sky transformed into an interesting chorus of blues and greys with streaks of silver and gold.

Eden turned onto C Street, the main street of her hometown. She never grew tired of its Old West feel. Some of the businesses she passed, had already been here for one hundred and fifty years. She especially loved the old schoolhouse. It was the last known historical school in the area. She continued to meander along the sidewalk, passing candy and ice cream stores, saloons and ghost hunting tour signs. As she

passed the Bucket of Blood Saloon, she saw
Wyatt standing in the shadows. He looked
moody and melancholic.

"Good morning, Wyatt. I heard you were on
the boat with Luke when he had his accident. Are
you both ok? I've been worried."

"Hello, Eden, I'm fine. I wasn't injured and
Luke is recovering well. He's at the lake house
with Cosette." Wyatt noticed Eden's face drop.
She looked sullen.

"Yeah, I heard. Seems like they are getting
kind of serious. They are basically living together
at this point."

"Nah, they are just friends. They aren't a good
match. Trust me," Wyatt responded confidently.
This perked up Eden's mood somewhat.

"Well, I need to get to work soon. I still have
some walking to do first. See you at the Watering
Trough tonight?"

"I have to work but I can swing by before my
shift." At that, Eden continued along her way.
She left the main road and headed to the
outskirts of town. She longed for some peace
and quiet before her shift started at the floral
shop. Once there, she would be inundated with

customer interactions all day, both tourists and locals. This was her last chance for solitude. She turned onto Cemetery Road. By now, the clouds had dissipated. A light, balmy breeze blew through Eden's hair. She loved the feeling of the fresh air on her sun kissed skin. She spotted two well fed robins up on a treetop. This brought a small smile to Eden's beautiful face. Their chirps came in bursts. They were clearly enjoying the new day. She passed a small meadow overflowing with fragrant flowers. She inhaled deeply and enjoyed the sweet aroma of peach blossoms.The grass was lush and a lonely brook babbled on the other side of the meadow. Yolk yellow ducklings loyally followed their mother into the water. Dragonflies whirred just above the surface of the water in a dance of life and death. Eden heard a whistle from the distance. At first, she assumed it was a bird. However, each whistle was different. The lack of consistency made it clear that this was whistling coming from a person. It continued but the sound appeared to be getting closer to her. The whistle began to take the form of do, re, mi, fa, sol, la, ti, do and then in reverse order. Eden felt a chill stir throughout her body. She picked up her walking speed, suddenly feeling desperate to get back to the safety of her home. Other than the whistling sound, there were no indicators of human life around her. She turned the corner around some well groomed hedges and saw him. He continued to whistle and smile at her. Eden felt a huge wave of relief.

"You scared me to death, silly." Instantly, she could sense something was different about him. His smile turned menacing. His eyes were uncharacteristically evil in appearance. His facial expressions reeked of complete insanity.Eden was completely caught off guard. This was not like how she knew him to be. "Is everything ok?" ,Eden asked cautiously.

"Oh, everything is more than ok, Eden." He began howling uncontrollably with laughter. "I thought I might find you here," he continued. Eden turned to run. She was the fastest on the track team in high school and she had continued to remain physically fit over the years. Her fight or flight response kicked in. Every instinct in her body was on high alert. She knew that she was in great danger. There was no doubt about it. Her shock and horror at the situation was overwhelming.

She felt his muscular hands roughly grab her forearm. His arm raised high above her and a shiny. large object glinted in the sunlight. Eden's entire world was instantly reduced to darkness. His laughter continued, even more satisfied and uproarious now. Minutes later, as he left her body there, he started whistling again and walked off to start his day.

"And what a wonderful day it already is". His body felt electrified. He was experiencing sheer and utter ecstasy.

Madison and Elizabeth were Sophomores at Virginia City High School. They were sitting in their last class of the day, German 2. They could hardly wait for the bell to ring. Finally, it blared out. They raced from their seats and entered the bright sunlight of the school yard.They were momentarily blinded by the intense afternoon sun.

"Finally," Elizabeth stated. "I thought that class was never going to end. We can walk home, at last." Madison chimed in with equal enthusiasm.

The two teenagers had been best friends since second grade. They were inseparable. In fact, they were next door neighbors. They had the pleasure of walking to and from school every day. It was just shy of a four mile distance from their homes to the high school but the best friends kept each other entertained. They rarely had a silent moment between them. The unforgiving desert sun blazed down on the young girls.The road ahead of them shimmered in the heat of the afternoon sun.Their only relief was when they occasionally passed under the shade of a tree. Molten gold beams splashed between the branches onto the sidewalk. Even with the slight breeze, the air remained thick and humid.

"This heat is more than I can take," complained Elizabeth. "Let's cut through the Quinn's meadow.That will save us at least five minutes. They are out of town this week." The girls took a sharp left and proceeded to walk through the fragrant, rolling hills of the meadow. The enormous oak tree gave them some reprieve from the unrelenting heat. Birds flew near them, diving hungrily for insects. A distant woodpecker kept a consistent beat as he worked to make a hole in a tree. The girls saw something off to the side of the meadow. Feeling curious, they walked over to it. The girls spotted a pool of blood encircling a lifeless woman. They both shrieked so intensely that the nearby birds startled and flew off of their branches.

"Oh my God, Madison! That's Eden Rose! She is obviously dead!" Terror filled their bodies. Eden's eyes stared vacantly into the distance. Elizabeth reached for her cell phone and dialed 911. She described their location and what they had discovered to the operator. The warm sounding operator calmed Elizabeth and told her that emergency vehicles would arrive at their location shortly. Both girls stood in the lonely meadow feeling frozen and, for once, speechless.They stared at Eden with wide eyes and shaking hands. Elizabeth tried to self soothe by wrapping her arms around herself. It did not work. Their terror only increased with each passing moment. They heard sirens racing towards them from the distance. Almost instantly, police cars and medics pulled in with screeching tires and they hastily parked parallel to the sidewalk.

The rest became a blur for the teenage friends. They were questioned and then sent away from the crime scene. The crime scene was roped off and processed. Eden had the telltale stiletto heel inserted into her throat. Law enforcement officers were dumbfounded. The killer had struck once again.

39

Due to the suspicious nature of Eden's death, a forensic pathologist was appointed to examine her post mortem. Stan Sillen had been a Medical Examiner for the past thirty-five years. He was known to be the best and most experienced in the state of Nevada. In fact, he had performed hundreds of autopsies on homicide victims over the years. Stan understood that a murder victim's body was generally the greatest source of invaluable and extensive clues in a crime. His primary mission was to help identify the cause of death and to collect trace evidence such as fibers, hairs or other materials which may have come from the murder weapon, the killer or the crime scene. He had become familiar with the rash of recent murder victims in the area. Stan had personally examined Maggie Hill, Lucy London, Harper Metcalf and now Eden Rose. He was certain, without a doubt, that these murders were committed by the same perpetrator. Each victim died from blunt force trauma with the same instrument and all had high heels placed into their throats. The angle of the instrument, height of the killer and even that the killer was left handed was unmistakable. Despite not yet beginning the autopsy, it was apparent that Eden met her end at the hands of the local serial killer.

Nina called Wyatt. He picked up the call on the first ring.

"Mr. Meier? This is Nina Sokolov. I am an agent with the FBI. I would like to set up a time to meet with you at the Virginia City station, as soon as possible." Wyatt sounded instantly guarded.

"What is this regarding?" ,he barked.

"I can explain everything when you meet with me. Could we meet within the hour?"

"Sure, that would be fine," Wyatt agreed, his voice sounded weary.

Forty-five minutes later, Wyatt was escorted to the interview room." He was surprised and somewhat relieved when he saw his lifelong friend, Jasper sitting at the conference table. A striking young woman greeted Wyatt with a handshake.

"I'm Nina Sokolov. Thank you for coming down to the station so quickly. Would it be ok if Sheriff Hopkins sat in on our interview?"

"That is fine."

Nina interviewed Wyatt for over three hours. He was cooperative and seemed open and truthful with his responses. Of course, he had no choice but to admit that he had recently bought his luxury car at the dealership in question. Some of his answers became inconsistent as the hours passed by. Nina excused him and thanked him for coming in.

After he left, Jasper admitted to Nina that he noticed the inconsistencies in his responses. He, however, insisted that his childhood friend would never be capable of committing such heinous acts. After some discussion, Jasper had other, more pressing ideas on his mind.

"Aren't we due to go out to dinner?" he asked flirtatiously as he pulled Nina into his arms. She loved to being so close to him. She inhaled his earthy aftershave.

"Now that sounds like a great idea, sir." She giggled and gently kissed his neck. Jasper's heart was pounding so hard that he was afraid she would be able to hear it. Nina made him feel delirious with desire. They wanted to enjoy an evening of privacy so they purposely avoided going to a restaurant on C Street. They went to an adorable Italian bistro on the edge of town. It was dimly lit and very romantic, complete with red checkered table cloths and flickering candle light.The couple was ushered to a small table in a dark corner. They pulled their chairs as close to each other as the furniture's legs would allow. Tasteful European artwork adorned the walls. Fresh flowers were perched in crystal vases on each table. Classical music chimed in the background. It all enhanced their amorous mood even more. Nina and Jasper could not keep their hands off of each other. An elderly gentleman seated at a nearby table asked them if they were on their honeymoon. They both giggled and blushed.

The wine flowed throughout the meal. Jasper held Nina close. They gazed in each other's eyes. Time stood still. They each felt a happiness they never knew they were capable of feeling. They savored their mushroom ravioli dish. It was one of the highest quality meals that had ever enjoyed. As much as they relished every moment of their time in the bistro, they both couldn't wait to go somewhere to spend some time alone.

After paying the check and leaving a generous tip, the couple departed from the restaurant and went to Jasper's car. He pulled her close and whispered in her ear.

"I do believe we have some unfinished business to take care of." Nina smiled and purred into his ear. She was in full agreement.

They went to Jasper's home. It was located on the edge of town. Nina enjoyed the rural feel of the residence. The front yard was encircled by a white picket fence. Jasper pulled his car into the detached garage. The home itself looked freshly painted in an antique grey color. They entered the home. It was small but very clean and well maintained. Nina loved it.

"Your home is so charming." Before Nina could continue speaking, Jasper wrapped his strong arms around her and held her close to him. They began to kiss passionately with an urgency neither one of them had encountered before. Nina trembled with delight. When Jasper looked into her eyes, she felt like he could see straight to her soul. Right then, Nina knew that even if she searched forever, she would never again find a connection like she had with him. Eternity did not even seem like enough time to spend with this incredible man. Her thoughts overwhelmed her but she knew it was true. Her skin erupted into goosebumps. Jasper devoured her mouth. His hunger for Nina had reached dangerous levels. The passion he felt for her made him feel weak. He felt as if he had been waiting for this moment his entire life. His hands dove into her luscious, silky hair. He pushed her gently against the wall and continued to kiss her furiously. He wedged his long, muscular thigh between hers. Nina felt she couldn't get close enough to him. They were both delirious with yearning and felt like wolves who hadn't eaten in weeks. A heat moved through them. They were speechless, close to mindless. Jasper couldn't stand the torment another minute. He picked her up effortlessly and carried her to his bedroom. She was feather light. He placed her gently onto his bed, kissing her the entire time.

The day dawned crisp and clear. The first rays of sunlight sprinkled into the room. Jasper and Nina had only been asleep for the past hour. They had just shared a night of unbridled passion together. Red lipstick and mascara smeared across one of the pillows. Two long stem champagne glasses were emptied on the nightstand. Jasper began to stir first. He woke up slowly and blinked away the rays of the sun. He looked over and smiled when he saw Nina fast asleep next to him. It wasn't a dream. The night had been everything he had hoped for and so much more. He felt an intense connection to her. His feelings for her were dizzying. He was overwhelmed by the speed in which his feelings had developed for her. He was a very lucky man. He treasured and adored her. He couldn't lose her now. Jasper padded to the kitchen to make a pot of steaming coffee in preparation for his lover's breakfast. He whipped up an omelet and poured two glasses of orange juice. Then he went to check on Nina. Jasper cuddled up close to her. He sighed when he felt the heat of her body. If they didn't leave for work soon, they'd never get out of bed. They both had a full day of meetings in front of them. He gently kissed her earlobe. Nina stirred. He held her closely to him. She sighed and felt giddy like a teenager.

"I never want this to end," she whispered in Jasper's ears.

40

Cosette jumped out of bed at the crack of dawn. She had been struggling to go back to sleep for hours. She lost the battle. It was useless to try to sleep because of the overwhelming excitement she was feeling. Today was the day she had been waiting for. She would finally see Spencer again.

The lake was drenched in the morning light. A lonely boat was bobbing in the distance. The seagulls were already diving into the frigid water to feast on their insect based breakfast. Cosette went out onto the deck. Most of the trees were still shrouded in darkness. Only the lake was basking in the sun's glow. The water was clear and glasslike. It was peaceful and statue still. A mob of flies ascended from the lake's surface into the air. The water called to her. Cosette peeled off her nightgown and ran down to the beach. She splashed into the frigid water. The soft sand mushed and squished around her toes. Her skin was rough with goosebumps. Cosette dove in head first and allowed the cold water to completely envelop her. Soon she noticed her limbs shaking. It was time to get out. Her body would not be able to take much more of the frosty lake.

Cosette ran up onto the deck. She buried herself under three layers of thick fleece blankets. She was amused and pleased by her new daring side. She had never been like this before. In the past, she would have refrained from even getting into a swimming pool if it was under 87 degrees. She smiled at the thought. She really had come a long way. Luke had changed her. She was always upbeat in the past but now she held even a stronger zest for life. Every day was a gift and she made sure to live each moment to the fullest. She took more risks.

She loved more fully and felt more passion than she had ever felt before. Cosette did not realize, until now, that she had just been going through the motions of living previously. Even her marriage to Chad felt obligatory because they only decided to get married once the pregnancy test had come back positive. They would never have gotten married if Cosette wasn't expecting Spencer. Spencer had been the only exception to her dreary past. She had loved him fiercely and unconditionally from the moment she gave birth to him. Other than her son, she had gone through life feeling very little happiness and excitement. Luke changed all that. He made her feel alive and happy. He was her true soulmate. Cosette believed this in every bone of her body. She sighed and sat back onto the outside daybed. She could see Luke descending down the stairs. He joined her out on the deck. His expression was sullen.

"Cosette," He approached her and sat next to her on the daybed. "I just received horrible news. Eden was found murdered." Cosette shrieked out and her skin instantly blanched,

"Oh my God! Where did it happen? At her home?"

"No, her body was discovered by two high schoolers on a field near the cemetery. Jasper called me and told me. He is convinced it is the same killer." Luke felt heartbroken. Although he had never been in love with Eden, they had a past together. He still considered her to be his good friend. They had even known each other since preschool. They had a long history. He felt gutted and he was frightened. He couldn't let anything happen to Cosette. Luke was dumbfounded that the killer had struck yet again. At that moment, he knew it was critical that he encourage Cosette, Spencer and her mother to stay here, with him, at the lake house. He needed to protect them, keep them out of harm's way. Cosette began to cry. Luke pulled her close to him. His heart ached to see her in pain. He whispered in her ear, "I'll never let anything happen to you, Cosette. I promise."

Cosette and Luke shared a quiet, somber morning together. They continued to hold each other and gaze out at the crystal lake. Although they were both feeling deeply melancholic because of the recent homicides, they felt a deep comfort in each other's arms. Both Luke and Cosette knew, within their own private thoughts, that they deeply loved each other. Neither could imagine living life without the other. Unfortunately, their feelings for each other still had not been expressed.

The time came to drive to the Reno airport. Spencer and Evelyn, Cosette's mother, would land soon. Luke and Cosette parked in the employee parking lot and waited at the baggage claim. Cosette felt overjoyed that she was about to get reunited with her son. Soon after, she spotted her mother and Spencer approaching. Spencer jumped into Cosette's arms. She twirled him around and they both felt jubilant. Then Evelyn and Spencer were introduced to Luke. The trio hit it off immediately. Cosette was secretly relieved that Luke was obviously a natural with children. Spencer and Luke were instantly at ease with one another. Evelyn was impressed by Luke's top notch manners and striking good looks. She noticed a look in Cosette's eyes. A look she had never seen before of love and pure happiness. Luke helped them with their baggage. The traffic was unexpectedly light and they soon arrived at the lake house. Evelyn was taken aback by the beauty of Luke's home. She had heard about the allure of Lake Tahoe in the past but it was even more breathtaking than she had imagined. Cosette showed her mother and Spencer to their rooms.

After they got settled in, they had a sumptuous lunch together. Luke barbecued chicken for them. They enjoyed hours of dipping in and out of the lake together. Cosette and Spencer threw a colorful beachball back and forth to each other in the shallows of the lake. The day was sunny and peaceful. The green grass of Luke's lawn lapped at the shimmering turquoise water. Evelyn lay in a hammock while reading a mystery novel. Luke sat on the edge of the dock and contently watched Cosette and Spencer playing in the gentle waves. His heart felt full of love and happiness. He enjoyed watching them. He knew how important it was for Cosette to spend time with Spencer. She had missed him immensely. As he suspected, she was a natural at being a mom. She was so loving, playful and patient. He went up to the kitchen and arranged a platter of ice cream bars.

"Dessert time."

"Yummy," Spencer called out and ran up onto the beach. "Can I have a drumstick, Luke?"

"You most certainly can," laughed Luke. After dessert, Luke gave Spencer two squirt guns. One was neon green in color. The other one was a vivid tangerine orange. Spencers eyes went wide with excitement.

"I love water guns. Thanks so much." Luke was touched by Spencer's gratitude. He was an endearing child. Spencer ran into the water and handed Cosette the tangerine colored one. The mother and son duo energetically played together, shooting each other with water and laughing uproariously the whole while. Minutes turned into hours.

Soon it was Spencer's bedtime. Evelyn decided to go to her room and rest as well. Cosette took Spencer up to his room. She had purchased a few children's books for him prior to his arrival. She tucked him in and was nine pages into the first book when Spencer drifted into a deep slumber. He was exhausted from traveling and playing in the water for hours. Cosette looked at him and smiled. Her baby was finally with her again. She soundlessly slipped out of his room and went downstairs and back outside to the deck. Luke was sitting on the outdoor bed. He had been waiting for her. He had even lit up the adjacent fire pit and poured two glasses of champagne. Cosette was taken aback by how particularly handsome he looked right at that moment. The firelight danced off of his perfect olive skin. It made her have to catch her breath. She felt like she was dreaming. Cosette sat down next to him and she noticed that he seemed hesitant.

"Is everything ok, Luke?" ,Cosette questioned somewhat alarmed.

"Everything is more than okay. I have been wanting to tell you something for a long time." He pulled her hands into his and continued. "I never knew when the right time to tell you this was. I came close to telling you several times already." Cosette's curiosity was piqued. "You mean a lot to me, Cosette."

"You mean a lot to me too, Luke." There was a moment of awkward silence.

"The truth is, I have been in love with you since pretty much our first date. I fought it at first because of your marriage but I can't deny it anymore. My every thought is consumed by you. I have never felt this way before, Cosette." Cosette's heart was galloping. She could not believe that he was confessing his love for her. Finally! She had been waiting for this for what seemed like her entire life.

"Oh, Luke, I feel the same way. I love you!"

"You do?"

"More than you will ever know," beamed Cosette. Luke moved in closer. Cosette felt his lips meet hers. His kisses felt so soft at first. Then they became more insistent, hungry and intense. He invaded all of her senses. The world stopped around them. His fingers curled desperately around hers. They both secretly peeked at each other a few times to make sure this wasn't just a glorious dream. Cosette's entire body tingled. Luke continued to come back in for more kisses, claiming her mouth countless times. His arms pulled her closer to him. His skin was smooth and radiated heat. Cosette had fantasized about kissing Luke many times. None

267

of her fantasies came anywhere close to how intense and perfect the reality was. Luke loved her and Spencer and her mother were both safely asleep inside. Life could not get better than this. She never wanted this day to end.

Months passed and the residents of Virginia City started to become less fixated on the homicides. Residents began to relax more. Most of the locals assumed that the murderer must have been a transient, after all, and he was now out of the area. Restaurants and bars filled up with locals once again. Nearby trails were finally in heavy use as they had been in the past. The town appeared to be completely reenergized.

Luke returned to live in his home in Virginia City and Cosette lived with Spencer and her mother at the cottage. Luke placed a top end security system on their cottage. He had pleaded for them to move into his home but she felt that, for the time being, it would be better to live alone with Spencer and her mother. He had enough to adjust to without having to deal with another man living with them.

Cosette enjoyed working as a flight attendant. Her schedule allowed her to work two days a week. The other five days, she spent with Spencer and Luke. On some evenings, Cosette helped Luke out at the Watering Trough. Romeo, the roadrunner, was considered a family member at this point. Both Cosette and Spencer were enamored with him. They fed him on a daily basis and he spent much of his time in their backyard. He even went directly up to their screen door and Spencer would feed him seeds from there. Cosette set up a bird bath in the garden. Romeo drank and splashed around in its cool depths. Luke had grown very attached to him as well. Life was good.

Local law enforcement was still working many hours a day on the four homicides. Nina continued to date Jasper. The FBI assigned her there until the murders were solved or the case was deemed cold, whichever came first. They were deeply in love and enjoyed every moment together. They had both been working long hours but when they finally got to spend time with each other, they were in a state of pure bliss.

Wyatt continued to work night shifts at the cemetery. He was more in love with Cosette than ever. It broke his heart and destroyed him to see her getting closer to Luke. They had announced two months ago that they were now an official couple. Wyatt went home and punched a wall. He curled up into a tight ball and wept. He was devastated. He put up a very believable act and pretended as if he were thrilled about their coupling. Wyatt continued to have meaningless flings with randoms tourists. He made a point of making Luke aware of his torrid one night stands. He bragged endlessly to his cousin about his nonstop escapades. He didn't want it to ever enter Luke's mind that his own cousin was madly in love with Cosette.

One night he met a sexy brunette at a bar in town. She introduced herself to him as Grace. She couldn't have been a day over the age of twenty-four. They shared a couple of gin and tonics. Then he invited her back to his place. They spent the night together. It was meaningless for Wyatt. He accidentally called out Cosette's name, at one point. Grace glared at him full of disgust,

"What did you just say?" He tried to redeem himself but she stormed off before he could get a sentence out. Her departure was a good thing in his mind. He was just going through the motions. After Grace left, he fell onto the bed and sobbed. He knew he was a very unhappy person. All these casual encounters with random women only made it worse. He wanted Cosette and only Cosette.

Grace left his place at about two in the morning. After her departure, he drove to Cosette's cottage. He couldn't help himself. His love for her sent him to the brink of insanity. He pulled up at the end of her street and parked. He quietly exited his car and walked along the isolated, lonely road. Owls hooted in the vicinity. The full moon basked happily in the sky above him. The stars looked like a blanket of crystals. The night was cloudless. He felt electrified to know he was so close to Cosette. He realized there was a chance he would find her sleeping in Luke's arms but he needed to see her. He soundlessly crept into her backyard, a location he had been to many times because of previous get togethers and when he had housesat for his cousin. He was familiar with every inch of this property. The branches in the garden became dancing silhouettes in the white-gold moonlight. The warm milky glow of the moon illuminated Wyatt's surroundings. Millions of stars were sprinkled in the distance. The dark shadows camouflaged the desert's nocturnal life.

He took a deep, cleansing breath of the crisp, earth scented air. Wyatt felt hypnotized by the bright, glowing orb in the night sky. It was all so mysterious. A wave of depression hit him. He needed her. The very thought scared him. He had never felt so sad and out of control in his entire life. In fact, around town, he had always been know as a playboy, a ladies' man. Cosette brought him to his knees. She made him feel helpless, like a newborn. He felt like he was slowly drowning in his own misery.

He crept over to her chest high bedroom window and he was relieved when he saw she had not drawn her curtains. Wyatt wasn't completely surprised. He knew how much she cherished looking for her roadrunner, Romeo, before bedtime. She also enjoyed the view of the desert. Cosette appeared to be in a deep sleep.

The nightlight located in the hallway was enough to give him a clear glimpse of her sleeping figure. To his relief, she was all alone. "Thank God." He had completely expected her to be wrapped protectively and territorially in his bastard cousin's arms. He continued to watch her with an extreme and painful longing. It shook him to his core. He pushed his face up against the spotless window and continued to stare at her through the glass, transfixed and mesmerized. Wyatt barely blinked. He was in a trance like state. Time became meaningless.

The most subtle of sun rays began to penetrate the garden. The sky changed from ebony black to golden hues. The sun bid the stars to take their nightly rest. The dawn was crisp and clear. Streams of light began to pour into Cosette's window. There was a pearly glow in the slowly lightening sky. A chorus of birds awoke, as if on cue, and began to sing the most melodious song. A rosy hue was cast across the desert sky. Dawn's first hawk took flight and soared above the sleepy town searching for its initial meal of the new day. The lush lawn was soggy with the morning's dew drops. A cool breeze caressed Wyatt's skin.He erupted into goose bumps. He knew it was time to depart. He had already pushed his luck by lurking this long in Cosette's garden. He thanked God that although the cottage was now heavily equipped with a top end security system, there was not a camera in place. His next night off was in five days. Wyatt vowed to himself that he would return to Cosette's bedroom window the first night which his schedule allowed. Just the very thought of seeing her would get him through the next week. He crept hypnotically off of the property and back to the safety of his ice cold car.

41

Nina was sitting at her desk at the Sheriff's office in Virginia City. She enjoyed the view she had of the main street from her window. The street was almost always littered with town locals and tourists. It was close to lunchtime. All morning Nina had been studying the killer profile which was written up by the Forensic Psychologist, Marie Johnson. She felt determined to solve the four homicides. It felt personal to her. She had been dedicating almost every waking moment to solving this perplexing case. Her sister's homicide, many years before, made her all the more determined to not give up until this monster was sitting behind bars. Her head sometimes spun as she reviewed the notes over and over again. She had every word in the various reports memorized, at this point.

Nina's nights were filled with nightmares about the faceless serial killer. She would wake up drenched in sweat and her heart pounded so hard that she could hear its beat. She was determined that nothing would stop her from figuring out who this killer was. In her desperation, she even wandered the lonely streets at night in hopes of baiting the killer in. None of her ploys worked. In fact, she never even got the slightest glimpse of anything suspicious going on. She was going to do it again tonight. Once darkness shrouded the town, she would don her highest heels, tightest, lowest cut top and mini skirt. She would strut in alleys in hopes of luring the killer to her. Of course, she never went anywhere without her trusted 9mm. It was tucked into a holder under her skirt.

Nina picked up lunch at a nearby deli. She ordered her usual, Reuben on rye sandwich. She devoured it at her desk, never letting her eyes wander from the various reports she was studying. After lunch she had a meeting with Detective Kelly Alexander. The ladies each took a mug of coffee into the conference room. They covered the table with countless papers about the case. Dr. Johnson joined them in the meeting shortly after. The three women had become an organized and hard working team. They would meet throughout the week to bounce off ideas to each other about the case. They were determined to not let it become a cold case. They felt that they owed it to the victims' families, friends and to the entire community. Wyatt often came up in discussions during their meetings. Kelly, in particular, felt it was too much of a coincidence that he had purchased a BMW recently from the exact same car dealership as the name stated on the business card which was found on one of the victims' body. Nina agreed that he was a person of interest in the case. She also felt that it was odd that not a single murder had occurred since Wyatt had been interview by the authorities a few months ago.

"Did he get spooked?" she wondered out loud to her colleagues. Kelly offered to trail him. Both Nina and Marie felt that was a great idea.

277

"Let's also ask him if he would be willing to come down to the station and take a polygraph test," suggested Marie.

"Great idea," Nina chimed in. "I will call Wyatt after our meeting." Nina reminded the ladies that although lie detector results cannot be used in a court of law, his results would at least give local law enforcement an idea if they were barking up the wrong tree.

"It certainly can't hurt," chimed in Kelly.

After the meeting was adjourned, Nina went back to her desk and called Wyatt's cell phone number. He picked up on the first ring and sounded breathless. After some initial pleasantries, Nina asked him if he would be willing to come down to the station and take a polygraph test. Her fingers were tightly crossed as she asked. Wyatt, without hesitation, declined to come in.

"I know how those tests can be," he replied abrasively. They aren't always accurate. I am not about to crucify myself." Nina could see that there was no point in arguing with him. She bid him goodbye and hung up the phone defeatedly.

Nina's afternoon consisted of going from one meeting directly into another one. She finally was able to call it a day shortly after seven in the evening. She went straight to Jasper's house. He greeted her with a long, warm kiss. Then she collapsed onto his sofa with a tired sigh.

"Long day?"Jasper inquired looking concerned.

"It sure was. I feel like we are dogs chasing our tails when it comes to solving these murders. Plus, Wyatt refused to take a polygraph. Every time I take a step forward, I take two steps back." Jasper pulled Nina close to his chest and said,

"I know just what you need, sweetheart. You need a night of relaxation and romance." Nina purred at the mere idea of it.

"Now that sounds like the best idea I have heard all day." She surrendered herself into his strong arms. Jasper called the local pizzeria and had their favorite, Hawaiian pizza and teriyaki chicken wings with ranch dressing, delivered. They enjoyed a night of feasting, cuddling and binge watching sitcoms. Nina was amazed how Jasper could make her forget all about her stress. Nobody had ever had the ability to do that in her past. A worry had recently began creeping into her mind. What if the FBI called her back to Quantico and she was forced to leave Virginia City? Jasper, so far, had not mentioned wanting a long term commitment with her. This scared her. In fact, he had confessed to her that he was "crazy about her" but he had yet to tell her that he actually loved her. She knew she was madly in love with him. She was not about to say the "L" word to him first. That just wasn't her style. Besides, she would never be able to show her face again if he didn't reciprocate her feelings. She would feel so humiliated.

Shortly after midnight, Jasper fell into a deep sleep. He was laying in Nina's arms. Nina held him tight. She felt his heart beating slowly and rhythmically. After she was certain that he was not going to be disturbed by her movements, she moved her arm out from under him. She waited a while, listening to his peaceful breathing. Then she lifted herself out of his bed and tip toed to the bathroom. Without turning on a light, she put on the outfit she had prepared. It would be described as sexy by anyone's standards. She donned a skin tight black mini skirt, a low cut, ruby red halter top and, to top off the outfit, she stepped into sky high, six inch stilettos. She looked into the mirror. It was only illuminated by a nightlight and she was impressed by what she saw. Her hair was silky and flowing flawlessly over her tanned shoulders. She was ready. Nina quietly left Jasper's house and emerged into the pitch black night.

She drove to C Street and parked. She sashayed down main street. The bars and restaurants were still full of people. A moment of panic swept over her. What would she tell Jasper if he woke up and found that she had left the house? She could always say that she received an urgent call from the Feds. The thought calmed her. She adored him and she did not want to ruin their relationship. Blaming her absence on her work seemed close to foolproof. There was no way he would be able to verify the validity of her excuse. She knew that the idea of flaunting herself on the streets in order to lure the serial killer in was highly unorthodox. However, this case was personal to her and she was willing to do things which she would not normally ever do in any other case. Her sister's murder was still a constant agonizing pain in her heart. Since her sister was killed by a serial killer, she became obsessed whenever she worked on cases involving serial killers. Nina would not rest until she caught this monster. It was as simple as that.

Wyatt was sitting in the Watering Trough trying to drink away his broken heart. He was on his fourth gin and tonic with a twist of lemon. Wyatt liked to buck the trend. Lime was a more common garnish to have with this type of cocktail. He liked lemon in his gin and tonic instead because yellow was his favorite color. His thoughts were consumed with Cosette. Every day he woke up in a deep depression and every night he fell asleep feeling just as low, all because of Cosette. He wanted her and he couldn't have her. It made him crazy. The feeling of the alcohol only caused him to feel even more melancholic. Nothing worked and he couldn't escape his misery. From his peripheral vision he noticed movement coming from the sidewalk. He was sitting next to the window. This allowed him a perfect view of the folks wandering the street. Wyatt's interest was piqued when he noticed a scantily clad, very well built woman passing by. Taking an anonymous woman home with him had been the only way he could distract himself from Cosette, at least for a few hours. He figured it was worth a shot. He closed out his tab for the night and quickly exited his cousin's establishment.

Nina turned onto a side street. It was dimly illuminated by just two faintly glowing street lanterns. The band music from a nearby bar was the only sound she still heard on this deserted lane. The music was growing softer with each step she took in the opposite direction. After a few minutes, she noticed a man approximately half a block behind her. Goosebumps erupted on her chilled skin. Nina did not speed up her steps. After all, her mission was to ultimately lure the killer of the four recent murders to her. She needed to make it easy for him. Her goal was to look as vulnerable and as helpless as possible. From Nina's experience, these vicious predators preferred targeting weaker and less physically intimidating women. It was critical that she played the part.

He was only about ten feet behind her now. His pace was quickening. Even though she was experienced in law enforcement, she still felt some anxiety during critical moments such as this. Her heart pounded and her palms were drenched in perspiration.

Suddenly the anonymous man clasped her shoulder roughly with his muscular hands and pushed her against the nearby dumpster. Her back seared with an intense, radiating pain on impact. She felt his mouth descend on hers. This was clearly an assault. She instantly grabbed her weapon and held it to his head.

"FBI, you are under arrest." The man froze. Before he even had time to react, she slapped handcuffs on him.

"What the hell?" the man hollered in his deep, shaken voice. Nina radioed for backup.

Once Nina was convinced that she had complete control over the situation, she aimed her high voltage flashlight at him.

"Wyatt Meier?" She knew he was already a person of interest in the area's rash of homicides, since he bought his BMW from the same dealership as the business card found on one of the murder victim's body. His eyes were wide with horror.

"This is all a big misunderstanding,",he insisted. Sirens wailed toward the alley. Within moments, the entire side street was teaming with law enforcement. Wyatt was read his rights and he was instantly taken into custody. Nina was elated. She was convinced that she had just single handedly arrested a serial killer. Wyatt was rushed to the Reno police department and booked. He was finger printed. The police were especially careful to follow the exact legal procedures. It was assumed that he was the area's serial killer. They did not want to taint this serious case. Wyatt did not make the process easy. He argued and fought with the authorities every step of the way. Finally, he was permitted to make one phone call. He called his cousin, Luke, and explained what had happened.

"Luke, I swear to you that I just wanted to make a pass at this woman. All I wanted was a one night stand. Everything went so wrong, so quickly. I am pretty sure that they think I am the killer. This is just ridiculous."

42

Although he had the intense pleasure of killing four women in the past year, he never felt quite satisfied. They all seemed too easy. These were not challenging murders. Each victim was caught off guard and barely fought back. It left him aching and hungry. After much contemplating and planning, he finally figured out what he needed to do to quench his thirst. He cleared his schedule for a few days. By doing this, nobody would be suspicious of his sudden absence from his job and from town. He knew the perfect next victim. She was everything he desired and then some. Contrary to the other slayings, he would abduct her and take her to a vacation home he had near the Mount Rose area. His cabin was only about forty minutes away from Virginia City. It was the ultimate home to fulfill this fantasies. It was a secluded home. There were no other neighbors within a quarter of a mile in either direction. She could scream at the top of her lungs and nobody could possibly hear her. The very thought relaxed and amused him. He was so ready to make his fantasies happen. Only one woman would do for his mission, the alluring Cosette DuPont. Half the fun would be seeing how much Cosette's death would destroy her adoring boyfriend, Luke. He desired more time with her than just a quick kill. Yes, the end result would be the same. He would end her life but not until he spent a few days making her life a living hell. She would beg for death to arrive. That feeling of power is what he needed. He was convinced that if he would be able to pull off this plan, he would, in fact, be satisfied for a much longer period of time.

Jasper awoke just as the morning light started pouring through the window. A steady patter of rain bounced lightly off of the roof. Thunder boomed directly above his home. He reached out to embrace Nina and he discovered he was alone in bed. He got up and began to call out for her. There was nothing but silence. Alarm began to rise in him. This was unlike Nina. He went to the kitchen to see if she had left a note on the refrigerator. There was nothing.

"Where is she?" ,he wondered out loud. He rang her cell phone. It went directly to her voice mail. He tried to contain his alarm. He jumped in the shower and briskly got ready to go down to his station. He continuously texted and called Nina. His nerves became increasingly frayed with each passing moment.

Only thirty minutes later, he arrived at work. He was greeted by Detective Alexander.

"We may have a crack in the case," she excitedly announced to Jasper. "Nina arrested Wyatt Meier during the night. He assaulted her in an alley." To say that Jasper felt stunned would be an enormous understatement. Why would Nina leave his home so discreetly during their night together. He felt hurt and confused. He responded to the detective.

"I grew up with Wyatt. I find it very unlikely that he is our serial killer." The detective explained that, at this point, he had only been arrested for assault. "They will now try to prove that he is also responsible for the four homicides as well. The feds are interviewing him now."

Luke's heart was broken that his cousin was arrested. He had no doubt that Wyatt would never be capable of killing someone. He knew that his cousin was good to the core. Luke assured him that he would immediately find the best attorney money could buy. After the cousins hung up, Luke immediately made a few phone calls. He hired the best attorney in the state of Nevada, Carson Swift. Cosette held Luke tightly in her arms. She could feel his high level of anxiety. He calmed somewhat in her loving embrace.

"I need to get down to the station and be there for him," Luke said in a shaky voice.

"Of course, Luke. Why don't I drop you off and then I'll go to the cottage to water the plants. You can just text me when you are ready to be picked up. I have quite a bit of gardening to do there today so don't rush. Wyatt needs you there."

"That sounds like a perfect plan. On the way home, we can swing by the market and pick up chops to grill tonight."

Not only was Luke crushed about his cousin's arrest but he had been planning for weeks to propose to Cosette tonight. His plan was to get down on his bended knee at sunset while sailing out in Emerald Bay. He had been so excited about it and had planned the proposal down to every last detail. He knew it would be inappropriate to propose to Cosette under the circumstances.

Cosette dropped Luke off at the station. She had rarely seen her boyfriend so tense. It hurt her to see him in any kind of emotional pain. She knew how close he was to his cousin. Wyatt's arrest had been torture for Luke. They kissed tenderly and then Cosette proceeded to the cottage.

It was hard not to cheer up when Cosette exited the back sliding door and her lively roadrunner greeted her full of enthusiasm.

"There you are, Romeo!" Cosette laughed at her own obvious excitement. She adored him. The sun was brutal on Cosette's skin. She was thankful that she had generously applied sunscreen before they had left the lake house. The desert sun was not forgiving. She had learned that lesson in the very first week of when she had moved to Virginia City. The heavy, distinct scent of honeysuckles invaded Cosette's senses. It overpowered most of the other scents in the garden except for occasional citrus notes from the orange tree. The garden overflowed with peonies, roses of various kinds and the welcoming white daisies. The sun overhead was a burning, amber colored orb. Cosette could hear the tranquil waterfall cascading onto the marble. It was rhythmic and soothing for her while she worked intently on the lush garden. Two wind chimes in the garden delicately broke the silence with their symphony as well. A hanging, colorful bird house remained constantly vacant. Cosette added seeds to the small porch of the bird house in hopes of encouraging a robin or finch to finally take up residence there. So far, her attempts had not been successful.

43

The tracker he had recently placed on the underside of Cosette's car had proven to be incredibly valuable. Up until this morning, she was constantly glued to her son, her mother, or to Luke. He was able to see that she had made a brief stop at the station and then she had continued on to the cottage. There was a chance that she wouldn't be at the cottage alone. He tried to remind himself that this may turn out to not be the day to fulfill his deepest, darkest fantasies after all. He would need to case the home. If she was, in fact, not alone, then he would need to abort his plans until another day.

He would be very disappointed but he could not afford to make any foolish mistakes at this point in the game. He pulled into the quiet lane and parked about thirty feet away from the cottage. Luckily, there were no nearby neighbors. It was a private street. The desert, with its various shrubs and brambles, was always ideal for him to conceal himself in. That he knew this property so well was, of course, an additional large bonus for him. He could not afford to be sloppy.

He exited his car silently, gently guiding the door closed. Looking intently around the vicinity again, he felt assured that there weren't any nosy individuals spying on him. He knew that the left side of the home was not fenced in. He darted quickly and soundlessly to the shaded area of the side yard. Momentarily, he paused behind the garbage bins. He listened intently. There was complete silence, as he had hoped. Theoretically, if Cosette was here with someone else, he would likely hear conversation. Silence is what he had hoped for. The surrounding desert was dotted with large rocks and sparse vegetation.The air was thick and arid. He continued to creep into the backyard. There she was, Cosette. She was concentrating intently on gardening. She used a shovel to disturb the soil. He simply stared at her for a while. He could not help but quietly sigh to himself. This was finally the day he had been waiting for. Once he felt confident that Cosette was, in fact, alone, he moved back to the front of the home and rang on the doorbell. It would be to his benefit if he didn't alarm her too early on in the process. The windows were open. The curtains swayed in the gentle breeze. He was certain she would be able to hear the front door chime from the garden. He rang the bell. Within a minute, he could see Cosette moving hesitantly to the front door. She saw him through the window and relaxed instantly because she recognized him. Even though she was perspiring from working in the desert sun, her beauty took his breath away. She swung the door open,

"This is a lovely surprise." Cosette was welcoming but seemed confused by his visit.

"I hate to barge in on you unannounced like this," he said pleasantly. "It's just that Luke has asked me to pick you up and bring you to him." Confusion crossed Cosette's pretty face.

"Is everything ok? I have my own car here. I can drive to him. I'll leave now." He did not plan on Cosette resisting his offer to drive. He foolishly assumed that she would go to his car with him without questioning the offer.

"I am happy to take you. Luke said he preferred that you ride with me," he persisted.

"I just don't understand. If I don't drive then Luke and I will be at the station without a car." Her resistance sparked a fire of fury within him. He expected her to be docile and submissive. This was already not going the way he had expected. He could feel beads of sweat forming on his brow.

"How dare she?" His pulse quickened. As Cosette reached for her purse and car keys, he went up behind her and threw her violently against the wall. She was knocked unconscious. He laughed triumphantly, "God, I am good at what I do. It is probably better this way. She could have caused a car accident if she would have been conscious in the car. Let her snooze until we get to my cabin. She will need her rest. I have an endless night in store for us!" Just then he heard her cell phone ping. It was Luke!

"Hi Sweetheart, I am done at the station. There's no rush. Please finish your gardening. I have missed you all morning. I love you!"

"Luke is such a fool! He thinks he misses her now. Ha! Little does he know that he will never see her alive again." He threw the phone off to the side, tied up Cosette, threw her over his shoulder and lay her down with a hard thump into his backseat. After scanning the surrounding area once more, he drove off, leaving Virginia City in the rear view mirror.

Luke waited anxiously for Cosette's response. At first, he remained calm when she didn't respond. He figured that she might be running the hose in the garden or doing some other task which made his incoming text impossible to hear. He sent another text to her about ten minutes later. There still was not a response from her. He called her cell phone number. After four rings, it went to her voicemail.

"How could she miss both my texts and a call? Her ringer was always on the highest volume." He asked Detective Alexander if she could drive him over to the cottage. They swiftly went to her car and she sped off to the lonely lane where the cottage was located.

Alarm bells sounded in both Luke and Detective Alexander's head when they reached the home and the front door was gaping open. Luke sprang out of the car before it came to a complete stop and raced into the cottage. He instantly saw that Cosette's cell phone was on the floor. This was particularly alarming because Cosette always took exceptional care of all her items. She was organized and clean. She would never toss her phone onto a floor. He went into the garden praying that she was safe and sound. As he entered the backyard, terror overtook him as he realized that other than Romeo, the garden was completely quiet. Cosette was nowhere to be seen. Terror gripped his heart. Sweat poured onto his forehead. The detective joined him in the garden moments later. Luke's voice quivered as he stated the obvious,

"Cosette's car is still parked out front. Her purse and cell phone are inside." Terror started to seal his throat. Detective Alexander tried to remain calm and think logically.

"Is it possible that she went somewhere on foot?"she suggested hopefully.

"I suppose it is possible but it seems very unlikely that she would leave the house without her purse, or at the very least her cell phone," The detective suggested that they drive around town.

"I wouldn't be surprised if it turns out she took a walk somewhere," she added optimistically. They patrolled every single street of the town more than once. Cosette was nowhere to be seen. The detective called the station and reported that Cosette DuPont was indeed missing.

As luck would have it, there was currently more law enforcement at the Virginia City Sheriff Station than there would have been in previous years because a lot of man power was being dedicated to finding the local serial killer. Since Maggie's murder, the station had been packed with detectives and FBI agents. Nina was immediately alerted of Cosette's disappearance. She had a horrible feeling that she may very well be the killers fifth known victim. Worry crisscrossed Nina's beautiful face. The trill of her cell phone interrupted her thoughts. She picked the call up on the first ring. The caller was Detective Alexander. She explained all the details of what she knew about Cosette's disappearance so far.

"I am going back to the cottage now to do a forensic investigation. Could we meet at about three this afternoon back at the station? We can review all of the evidence we have collected," suggested Detective Alexander.

"Yes, I will be there. Thank you so much for the update. We need to find her. Time is of the essence, if it isn't too late already," Nina's voice quivered. Nina hung up and looked down at her clothes. She was still in the provocative outfit she wore the night before when they arrested Wyatt. Her ridiculous high heels were making the soles of her feet scream out in pain. She needed to shower and change before she attended that important meeting later this afternoon. She also felt bad for not responding to Jasper's concerned texts. She had been inundated with work and had literally not found a moment to respond to him. She needed to apologize to him. She would go to his home, talk to him and beg for his forgiveness. Then she would shower and wear her favorite suit, the powder blue one. It was hanging, freshly ironed, in Jasper's closet.

She arrived at Jasper's home soon after. She knocked and he didn't respond. She had her own key to get into the residence. She felt giddy when he had surprised her with her own key recently. Nina was deeply in love with him and she was hoping that they would eventually get engaged. She entered the residence and called out his name a few times. There was no response. Sadly, she would need to postpone her apology to him for now. Nina turned on the rain jet shower to the highest temperature. She placed her clothes neatly on the counter and entered the steamy paradise. She had left her favorite body wash there, the olive and green tea scented one. It relaxed her muscles. She ached to go to sleep but she knew that she needed to get ready for her meeting. She would have to sleep after the meeting.

She toweled off and slipped into her magenta colored, terry cloth robe. Nina's stomach rumbled impatiently. She suddenly realized that she had not even stopped to eat since around two in the morning. No wonder she was famished. She padded to the kitchen and could see that Jasper must have left the house in a hurry. Dishes and pans were piled up haphazardly. She couldn't help but smile. Jasper had countless wonderful qualities but cleanliness was not one of them. She made herself a gooey, mozzarella grilled cheese sandwich on seven grain bread. Then she placed the dishes into the dishwasher and started the heavy duty cycle.

"Ok, that's done. Now I need to get my suit." She entered Jasper's walk in closet and spotted her favorite suit. She had a tailor, custom fit it, for her specific measurements. She had to admit, that it showed off her svelte figure perfectly. The color of the suit also highlighted her crystal blue eyes. She admired herself in the full length mirror. As she exited the master bedroom to find her heels, she clipped the belt loop of her skirt onto the strike plate of the door. It was a jagged metal piece located on the side where the door closed. This piece had always protruded more than it ideally should have. Jasper's house was an older, vintage home. The protruding strike plate was one feature he had been meaning to upgrade for months. To Nina's dismay, not only had the belt loop ripped but the skirt's thread had been slightly pulled.

"I cannot believe this, of all the days for this to happen and I don't have an extra suit at Jasper's house. He must have a sewing box around here somewhere. It should take me less than five minutes to repair the skirt" Nina looked for a sewing box in all of the obvious places first. She looked from top to bottom in the laundry room and in the bathroom. "My mom always keeps her kit in the closet. Maybe it is in there." Upon initial inspection, Nina did not see anything which looked like a sewing box. She was determined to find one. She couldn't show up at a meeting looking disheveled. Then she noticed a nondescript, white box stashed in the corner of the closet behind a pile of Jasper's sweaters. She almost missed seeing the box but the corner protruded slightly out from the sweaters.

"This must be it," she thought feeling relieved. She moved Jasper's sweaters to the side and pulled the box down. Nina transported the box to the master bed. "The lighting is way better in here than in the closet for sewing anyway." She lifted the lid and, at first, she felt confused by its contents. "Well, this definitely isn't a sewing kit."

The box was full of gadgets. At first, the gadgets appeared to have no rhyme or reason. She saw snips of hair and newspaper clippings from the local serial killings. Initially, Nina tried to remain calm. She told herself that there must be a reasonable explanation that Jasper had a box such as this. After all, he is the sheriff of the town. It would make sense that he would closely monitor the newspaper articles. However, as she looked deeper into the box she knew she couldn't fool herself anymore. Sheer horror overtook her. She found a necklace with an "M" pendant. She remembered that Maggie always wore a necklace just like this one and it had been missing since her slaying. Cold sweat formed on her brow. Fear and sadness tore through her gut like a slicing blade. She fought a rising panic within her. She trembled inside. She felt her entire body get weighed down by, not only fear, but extreme emotional pain. She shivered but continued to inspect every item in the box. Nina found photos of not only the four women but also many other women, not connected to the local killings. Each photograph was clearly taken of the victim post mortem. There were also countless hair samples wrapped in scarlet red ribbons. Nina estimated that there must have been at least forty different hair samples. Her world came crashing down around her. The future she had been dreaming of was deleted right before her very eyes.The contents in this box were unmistakable. Jasper, the man she was in a relationship with and dreamt of marrying one day, was the local serial killer and from the looks of it, he had murdered many other women besides the four local ladies. Nina felt dizzy. Her stomach cramped. As a woman and as his significant other, she was crushed but she was also an FBI agent. She couldn't save her own sister many years ago but she had the power to possibly still save Cosette DuPont, if it wasn't too late.

44

Cosette's eyes blurred. She was confused and her head was throbbing. She felt dizzy and weak. A radio was blaring. Soon she realized that the rhythmic movement she was feeling was a moving car. "Where was she?"

Finally, her eyes were able to focus. She spotted dark brown leather seats. Trees seemed to race by her as she peered outside of the dusty car window. The world was moving past her at lightning speed. Fear engulfed her. The duct tape stuck painfully to her wrists and ankles. It felt as if rashes were beginning to form on her skin and her forearms burned. She tried to pull out of her confines but it was useless. Her legs cramped.

"Well, hello, sleepy head," a loud, masculine voice boomed from the driver's seat. Her memory flooded back.

"Jasper!" He had abducted her. But he was the sheriff of the town. He was even friends with Luke. "What on earth was going on?" Cosette wondered. "What do you want with me, Jasper?" Cosette demanded.

Her question caused Jasper to roar in laughter.

"It would be a shorter list to tell you what I don't want from you," he answered in the most chilling, creepy voice that Cosette had ever heard in her life. Her heart leaped into her throat. She wanted to be with Luke and her son. They must both be sick with worry about her by now. This was an indescribable nightmare. She needed to find a way to get away from this sociopath. Fear fluttered in Cosette's heart.

She remained quiet for the rest of the ride, calculating an escape. Her palms were so clammy that she had hoped that the moisture would loosen the tape. Unfortunately, she was not that lucky. Cosette was forced to be close to motionless with all the duct tape he placed on her.

"Here we are, my beautiful angel. Welcome to our honeymoon." Cosette gasped in horror. Jasper parked the car with a jolt and pulled her like a sack of potatoes out of the back seat of his car. Cosette quickly tried to memorize every detail of the surroundings. It could end up being useful if and when she was finally able to escape. They were located in a thick forest on a mountain. The trees were mahogany brown in color. The Sierra Mountain's seasons had been harsh to the bark of the trees, stripping away and tattering them. Songs of nearby birds came in bursts and lulls. Cosette could detect the sound of moving water in the distance. The property was deeply shaded by Washoe Pines, a rare type of pine tree which only exists in the Reno area. A handful of sunlight rays managed to glint through the thick, majestic trees. The deep, damp brown earth was covered in pine cones of varying sizes. Standing before her was a modest looking cabin. As Jasper carried her to the front door, she could hear twigs crunching under his feet. He brutally kicked open the front door and bounded into the cabin while holding Cosette in his clutches. He threw her roughly onto a tattered, stained, olive green futon. The air in the room was stale, almost nauseating. The room was pitch dark due to the thick black out curtains on all of the windows. Cosette wondered if he had used this cabin to abduct other women in the past. It was the ultimate location for complete privacy. Horror filled Cosette's heart.

"Think! Where would Jasper take Cosette?" Nina pushed herself to come up with a plan to locate the missing woman. She knew that time was of the essence. Nina was a highly trained FBI agent. She even specialized in serial killings. She thought back to the many conversations she had with Jasper. There would be clues somewhere during the span of their relationship. Nina suddenly remembered that Jasper kept photo albums in his dresser drawers. She pulled all four of the albums out. Two of them were from his childhood. The other two were from his adulthood. She saw photos of when he had graduated from the police academy. Years prior to his graduation from police academy, there were photos of when he had worked as a long haul trucker. He stood in front of at least a dozen different "Welcome" signs from different states. He smiled proudly from his shiny, red big rig. Then she saw photos which jarred her memory. Jasper was standing in front of his vacation home on Mount Rose. He was fishing at a location near his cabin in another photo. It had completely slipped her mind that he had a second home. He rarely mentioned it.

"That had to be it. He had been missing in action for the majority of the day. If he had already killed Cosette he would have gone right back to his daily routine but since he had been radio silent, he might have brought the poor woman up to that cabin."

Nina needed to do something. She called Luke and filled him in. She told him about the box she had discovered in Jasper's closet. After an initial brief period of being in shock that his lifelong friend was indeed a serial killer, he became close to hysterical with fear at the thought of Cosette being in potential mortal danger. After she hung up with Luke, Nina called and updated the detectives at the station. They were all briefed on the address of Jasper's vacation home. An all points bulletin was put out. There was a mad rush to arrive at the mountain home.

45

Cosette sat in a tangled mess on the sofa. She felt utterly uncomfortable and she felt more scared than she had ever felt in her life. She had often heard that people know when they are about to die. Cosette had this horrifying feeling that her time was almost up. She sensed that she was going to die soon. The mere thought sent shivers of horror up and down her spine. Cosette wasn't ready to leave this earth yet. She needed to be here for her young son and she was waiting for the moment that she would become Luke's wife. Her time couldn't possibly be up, she thought desperately. Jasper stood at the foot of the futon and stared down at her with evil and soulless eyes. He glared at her without blinking and than began to speak to her.

"I have been dreaming of the day I would get you here. Do you realize that I have complete power over your life and death, Cosette?" He spit the words out similar to a venomous serpent. Cosette stared at him in complete horror. She couldn't believe she was here in this mountain cabin with him. She was powerless and separated from everyone she loved. Her eyes brimmed with tears. Then a horrible thought came to her and she asked him,

"Did you kill my best friend, Maggie and the other women?" Cosette's voice quivered.

"Wow, you really are a genius! Ding! Ding! Ding! You win the trip to Jamaica." Jasper howled with laughter. His eyes even teared from his hysterical laughing fit. Cosette stared at him with sheer terror in her eyes.

"Of course, I killed them. All four of them. Heck, they were just an appetizer. I killed several dozen women before them. Leaving my transcontinental trucking job and having to come back to Virginia City to take over my dad's position as the sheriff when he retired truly cramped my style. For years, I have had to hold it together, more or less." He laughed heartily again.

"But, why,"Cosette pleaded?

"I will tell you why. Women are disrespectful to me. They always have been. I got screwed over when my mom abandoned my dad and me when I was only six years old and every woman since then has betrayed me. Each and every one of you deserves what you get. Your precious Luke is the biggest jerk of all. I was crazy about his ex, Eden. She never gave me the time of day because she was still hung up on that bastard. I taught her a lesson. He seems to truly love you. What better way to mess with his head than to murder you too? It's a win win. I delete another woman from this world and I destroy the ultra popular, Luke Meier." Cosette desperately tried to reason with him.

"But you will get caught. Do you really want to spend the rest of your life behind bars? Also, you are in a relationship with Nina. She obviously adores you."

"Leave Nina out of this,"Jasper hissed. She is the greatest woman I have ever known but clearly it will just be a matter of time before she burns me too and I definitely will end up behind bars, or even worse, if I don't kill you. You are the only who knows that I am the killer. Killing you will only buy me more time. Nobody would every suspect me. I am the sheriff, an upstanding, well liked citizen." Cosette stared at him with sad, wide eyes. She had never felt such intense terror. Looking in his eyes, it was clear that this man was pure evil. Reasoning with him would be of no use. She needed to figure out an escape plan.

Luke and Detective Alexander raced along the windy mountain road. The GPS indicated that they were about ten minutes away from Jasper's vacation home. They opted not to take a helicopter since it would alert Jasper that law enforcement was close by. Luke's heart was pounding. He did not think he would be able to survive if Cosette was injured or even worse. The mere thought of it made his heart ache. The forest was getting thicker, the higher up they went in altitude. The ground amongst the trees looked like a deep green carpet. Thick, knotted tree roots glided in and out of the forest floor. The smell of pine trees mixed with the distinct smell of wet earth wafted through the open windows. Rays of wheat colored sunlight filtered through the dense canopy of trees. Luke spotted birds dancing joyously among the tree branches and a small creek gurgled in the distance. Squirrels rustled in the foliage. The serene environment did not match Luke's mood. It took every ounce of strength to control the rising panic within him.

The detective parked about a quarter of a mile away from Jasper's home in hopes of not making their presence known to him. Luke and the detective were grateful for the many hiding places the forest provided them with. Both of them were armed with fully loaded Glock 22s. Luke spotted the home in the distance. Soundlessly, they made their way to the shrubbery located not far from a side entrance. Minutes later, seven more law enforcement officials arrived at the scene. They all parked in the distance as well and discreetly joined Luke and Detective Alexander. Officer Josh Barton had arrived at the scene with a detailed outline of the floor plan of Jasper's home. After some deliberation, they decided that negotiating with this psychopath would only put Cosette's life in grave danger. They needed to storm the house with no warning whatsoever. Since the curtains were all closed, Jasper would presumably not be able to see them through the windows. A back door which connected to the deck seemed less secure than the front door. The back door would allow law enforcement to immediately enter the family room. Three agents planned to enter through the back door. The remainder of law enforcement would enter through the side door. This was a high risk procedure because there was no way to know where Cosette and Jasper were located in the home. It had to be done quickly. Jasper's other four known victims were murdered by him soon after he had them under his control. There was, in fact, a high likelihood that Cosette was no longer alive.

Both groups of officers lined along their respective doors, their guns were in hand. Timed to the second, both groups busted through the doors with battering rams. They stormed the residence. Luke was asked to not take part in the raid since he was not law enforcement. He refused to listen and entered the back door less than thirty-seconds after the officers had entered. A terrified Cosette was bound in an abundance of duct tape and she was located on the futon. Jasper lunged for her but Officer Alexander grabbed him and cuffed him before he could even reach his tormented hostage. Luke ran to Cosette and began to undo her bindings. She was crying hysterically with a mixture of stress and relief. Jasper was read his rights and arrested. He resisted and rambled furiously to Cosette that he would spend every minute of every day for the rest of his life plotting how to find her and finish the work he had intended to do with her.

"You are dreaming if you think this is the last you've seen of me, Cosette. An arrest won't keep me away from you. I will get you when you least expect it." He roared out loud with his insane and evil laughter. Luke began to lunge at him and before Luke could come into contact with him, Jasper was roughly pulled out of his home and into a squad car. Cosette collapsed into Luke's arms.

"I thought I was about to die. I was sure I would never see you or Spencer again." Luke pulled her close to him.

"I will protect you now and forever. I will never let anyone hurt you again, sweetheart," Luke vowed.

46

After Jasper's arrest, there was a great deal of shock and grief in town that one of their most beloved citizens was indeed a serial killer. Jasper's former schoolmates, friends and family members deeply mourned that the man they knew and loved was, in actuality, a very evil man. Nina, in particular, was heartbroken. After tying up some loose ends with the case, she moved away from Virginia City and went back to Quantico with a very heavy heart. She thought Jasper would one day be her husband and the father of her children. She tried to remind herself that she accomplished what she had come to this area to do, solve a serial killer case and remove a murderer from the streets. Nina just hadn't expected the killer to be a man she had fallen deeply in love with. She felt like such a fool. Particularly as an FBI agent, how could she not have picked up on any signs that he, in fact, was a killer? Sadly, it would be a very long time, if ever, that she would be able to trust another man again.

After some time, Cosette was able to heal somewhat from the horrible trauma Jasper had put her through. She continued to work as a flight attendant and she spent all of her free time with Spencer and Luke. Life was starting to return to normal in the small, close knit town. Residents began to feel safe again now that there was no longer a killer on the loose.

It was a glorious spring afternoon. Cosette, Luke and Spencer were driving in the convertible. They all felt more relaxed than they had in a long time. Virginia City was beautiful in every season but Cosette particularly enjoyed it during the spring time. The weather was so fresh and warm. A breeze of succulent, fragranced flower petals whipped at their skin. The sky was etherial blue in color and completely cloudless. They arrived at the cottage to do some gardening.

"I can't wait to see Romeo," Spencer exclaimed.

"I can't either, Spencer," Cosette agreed. The trio entered the home and went into the backyard with their watering cans, seeds and buckets. Romeo was nowhere to be seen.

"I have noticed he often seems attracted to our backyard when the hose lightly runs. He is drawn to the flowing water. I will turn on the faucet," Luke offered. Luke slowly turned the faucet handle onto the on position while Cosette and Spencer placed Romeo's favorite seeds in his feeding area. They started to garden. Cosette brought out icy lemonades for her two favorite people in the world. The desert sun was baking all of them.

Shortly after, Cosette could hear Romeo's distinct call. "Co-Coo-Coo-Coooo" Within seconds he bounded into the garden. Cosette was startled when she saw him. Something was wrong with his gait and he seemed to be in distress. He stumbled towards her while holding his left wing.

"Luke, something is wrong with Romeo!" Cosette called.Luke and Spencer came over to inspect. Since Luke had lived in desert terrain his entire life, he was very familiar with roadrunners.

"Oh no. It looks like he has a broken wing," Cosette gasped in despair.

"Let's take him to the vet. Hopefully they can do something to help him,"Luke suggested. Spencer found a comfortable, roomy box to place their beloved bird into and then they went briskly to the town vet. Dr. Jensen, an elderly and highly experienced veterinarian, greeted them warmly and inspected Romeo in a small examination room. Upon careful examination, he gave his opinion.

"I have good news and bad news. His wing can be fixed. I will need to wrap his wing in a way that ensures that the bones are correctly aligned. He will be limited in movement in order to prevent his wing from coming out of alignment."

"That is great news," Cosette gushed with a wave of relief. She inquired, "What is the bad news?"

"He will not be able to be released into the wild until the wing is completely healed. Even, at that point, there is a fairly good chance that it will not be safe for him to be released back into his habitat." Luke spoke up before Cosette could even respond to the kind hearted veterinarian.

"That is not a problem, Dr. Jensen. We have grown very attached to Romeo. I can build a large enclosure on my property. We will take care of him indefinitely." Cosette beamed at Luke. She felt touched by his generous offer. He knew how much she loved Romeo.

Just two weeks later, Cosette was at Luke's home. She was out on the pool deck surrounded by Spencer, Romeo and Luke. The sun began to set over the desert. They enjoyed a tasty barbecue and swam in the pool. Cosette rested on the outdoor bed with a glass of champagne in her hand. Luke and Spencer walked over to her. She startled when Luke got down on one knee. He proposed to her and Spencer even handed Cosette the ring. Cosette could not say yes to Luke's proposal quickly enough. They both cried tears of joy. They had been through so much together such as the pain of the four ladies' slayings and discovering that a close friend, Jasper, was actually the monstrous serial killer. As horrible as that period had been, it had only made their bond stronger. They were excited and ecstatic to spend the rest of their lives together as a family.

47

The house sat at the end of a quiet road. Some of its windows were boarded up. The residence looked grey, gloomy and unwelcoming. The front yard was unkempt. Weeds and unruly wildflowers had overtaken the front lawn. The children in the neighborhood were convinced that it was a haunted house. The annual parade of trick or treaters had an unspoken understanding to never knock on this home's door. A thick layer of dust had accumulated onto the creaky front door. Inside, the air was dry and reeked of stale smoke. The windows were never opened to allow much needed fresh air inside.

He sat reclined in the lounger in his family room. The wind was howling outside, causing the shutters to rattle and whine. The curtains were thick and completely prevented any light from entering. The only illumination in the room was the glare coming off of the computer screen. His pale green eyes fixated on an article of the latest serial killer arrest. He reclined in his chair while puffing hungrily at his favorite cigarettes, Marlboro. The rings of smoke twirled heavenward. His walls were covered with years of news clippings from countless serial killers, their arrests and their delicious murders. The Virginia City's serial killer's recent arrest was splashed all over the news and social media. He had mixed feelings about Jasper's apprehension. He had enjoyed reading about the killings. They were beautifully executed and meticulously completed. This most recent killer had become one of his heroes. He learned a great deal from all of the serial killers. Their arrests always disappointed him. He was their biggest fan and he rooted for them. The one positive thing which came from their eventual arrests was that he learned what not to do. The time was now. He had been waiting for this moment since his childhood. Of course, he had been practicing torturing for years on small animals but he was finally ready to start killing people. The mere idea of ending human lives made him feel breathless and intoxicated. The feeling of complete power over another person's life left him giddy and ecstatic. He had been very patient. Up until now, he never believed he was organized and skilled enough to be an effective killer. He finally felt properly trained and ready. He went onto his Facebook page and surveyed all of his Facebook friends. Several women seemed as if they would make an ideal first victim for him. His attention became particularly captured by one of his friends, Tinsley. "My, isn't she just perfect for what I have in mind!"

"Let the games begin," he thought with a confident and triumphant chuckle.

To my son, Jason, for his tireless commitment to editing, cover design and technical support.

To my daughter, Sara, for motivating me with her supportive words and upbeat, warm nature.

To my daughter, Olivia, for her thoughtful writing advice and whose exceptional talent in photography created the book cover.

To my daughter, Lauren, who patiently brainstormed ideas for the book's content and was the model for the cover.

To my husband, Mark, for having an uplifting sense of humor throughout the process and providing support and guidance.

To my brother, Christian Hofstadter, for editing and being an unbeatable confidant to me, not just during the process of writing, but always.

The Stalker in the Desert would not have been possible without the love and support of each and every one of you.

Printed in Great Britain
by Amazon